I0663848

ZOMOPOLIS

by

R.G. Hart

53RD STREET PUBLISHING

Praise for R.G. Hart's "My Partner the Zombie" in the zombie romance anthology, *Hungry For Your Love* from St Martin's Press

"Filled with stories from the hilarious to the horrific ... there is something here to tug at the hearts (and brains) of any zombie lover. Highly recommended for anyone's collection." — Monsterlibrarian.com"

"Unrequited love is hard to accept, but Aloha Armstrong knows that she has only herself to blame.

"Being a Zombie is not an easy existence, but Matt Butcher is resigned to making it the best it can be.

Following up on a story of attempted murder puts Matt and Aloha in the path of a madman. They must ferret out the truth before more people are infected with the virus. Aloha wants the man caught, but she is devastated that she could very well lose Matt in the process.

There is a great dynamic between Matt and Aloha, and it really makes for some fun reading." http://coffeetimeromance. com/BookReviews/hungryforyourlove.html — Coffee Time Romance — (4 cups)"

"A wonderfully twisted undertaking (pun intended), 'Hungry for Your Love' is a many-faceted feast of love, loss, sex, heartbreak, rotting flesh, and romance from beyond the grave." — Christopher Golden, bestselling author and editor of *The New Dead*"

Zomopolis
Copyright 2012 by R.G.Hart
All rights reserved

Cover Artist:
Nuno Moreira
Cover Photo by:
ThomFoto/IStockphoto
Logo image by:
Engraver | Dreamstime.com
ISBN 978-1-927621-13-4

Published by 53rd Street Publishing
Also available in E-book

Dedication

This one is for Kris and Dean, two excellent writers, teachers, mentors and most importantly, friends.

Acknowledgments

A good story well told becomes a better story with a talented editor. Many thanks to my editor, Cindie Geddes at Lucky Bat Books. This book owes as much credit to Cindie as it does to me, she helped elevate the words on the page to new heights. Thanks, Cindie.

Nuno, you rock! Thanks.

And of course I must thank, Rita who is steadfast in her support and love. Thanks, my dove.

Chapter One

*H*E LOOKS HUNGRY.
Suddenly the lurching zombie snatched the ham steak off the plate on the lunch counter, then, with its gray fingers, stuffed the dripping piece of meat whole into its mouth. It chewed noisily as a line of drool ran from the side of its mouth down its cheek.

Yup, he's hungry, all right.

Sheriff Aloha Armstrong's brow wrinkled in a wince of revulsion. She took a single cautious step closer to the zombie. What was he doing in here?

Then again, here I am an undercover Legal Investigative Protection agent stuck in the great wet Northwest. L.I.P.S. agents were supposed to work in warmer climes like Florida or California. At least that was what the recruitment brochure said when she signed on six years ago. This latest assignment had led her to Zomopolis, a small town situated in a remote valley halfway between Spokane and Seattle so it rained a lot. Thankfully the town was constructed under a dome so weather wasn't an issue; otherwise she would have quit on day one. Too many days of rain depressed her. *What's a secret agent gal who loves to suntan to do?*

1

Aloha watched the zombie.

Everyone knew brain-eaters ate at Cerebellum Station, the Brain-Eater-Only cafe that specialized in brain food. Joe's Family Diner didn't serve their kind — only living humans not undead ones.

Aloha winced and immediately scolded herself. *What am I thinking? Their kind?* Some of her best friends were zombies.

Like too many times before, the memory of her ex-boyfriend, handsome former-zombie, Matt Butcher, popped into her mind. *Man, I wish I could get that guy outta my hair, and my subconscious.*

Her stomach muscles tightened. She took in a deep breath and held it, causing her ample bosom to swell. Out of the corner of one eye she spied 90-year-old Mr. McDok staring at her from where he lounged in a red leather booth. His weathered features were split by a salacious grin. Not that this surprised her, since the form-fitting sheriff's uniform did little to hide her voluptuous figure. She scowled at him. He was a dirty old man.

She decided she had to make time to fix her uniform. She'd been too busy settling into the new routine of the job. It seemed sheriffing was harder than secret agenting.

Shifting her attention back to the ham-munching zombie, she released the air from her lungs as quietly as possible so as not to alert the brain-eater to her presence.

Her deputy, Elvis Bushwood, had already herded the diner's customers, except McDok, who refused to leave the booth, through the kitchen and out the back door of the diner.

Elvis's round, nut-brown, hairless head and beady brown eyes filled the small window of the swinging door that separated the counter area from the kitchen.

From the way Aloha's police-issue boots (about as ugly a piece of footwear as ever invented) slipped with each step she took she knew the floor tiles' checkerboard had been freshly waxed this morning. Disregarding her own safety, she ever so slowly edged closer and closer to the zombie. She didn't want to have to kill a local one week into the job, but he had to be stopped before he ate the brain of a live human. The undead living amongst the not-dead still irked her, but the town of Zomopolis was what it was.

At the job interview, the mayor had been adamant about not shooting the town's zombie residents. Mayor Sharona Figer explained the local economy was dependent on good relations between the living and the undead. The mayor explained the living people in the town were from all across America, the best and brightest working on a foolproof cure for the zombies. Aloha's job was to protect them and prevent crime.

Aloha tipped her head to the side as a signal to Elvis to come through the door. He blinked twice and swiveled his neck as if to get out a kink but didn't move to enter. Elvis had the Legal Investigative Protection Service net gun she'd given him earlier. The brilliant Dr. Oh, chief R&D scientist at the L.I.P.S. weapons laboratory, had been proud of the gun's intimidating look, but Aloha was unimpressed with it. According to Dr. Oh, the gun had an effective range of only five feet, and unless Elvis came through the door she would have to face the zombie alone. Which meant, of course, she'd have to shoot it.

Her plan was to block the zombie's escape out the front door while Elvis trapped him with the net gun. Aloha would provide the frontal assault and scare the brain-eater toward Elvis.

It was the classic pincher strategy perfected by Napoleon over 300 years ago.

C'mon, Elvis. Move!

But he stayed still, staring uncomprehendingly at her through the door's tiny window.

She hoped he understood SWAT-talk. She raised one arm and used it to signal he was to come into the counter area. He shook his head.

She sighed. *He doesn't understand SWAT-speak? Where did he receive his police training, the school for small-town cops?*

Next, she pointed at him, then at herself, then at the zombie. Finally she showed three fingers, hoping to indicate on the count of three they would make their move on the zombie. This time Elvis smiled and nodded. *Good, finally he gets it.*

Suddenly her left foot slipped on the tiles, making a loud scraping noise like fingernails on a chalkboard. She froze with her legs wide apart, trying to keep from falling. Her upper body swayed back and forth while she waved her arms like wings in an attempt to stabilize herself. *Whoa!*

That was too close.

Her heart was racing when the zombie turned around to face her. A sliver of drool ran from the left side of his undead mouth, and his ink-black staring eyes were free of any trace of human emotion. His blond hair was cut jaggedly as if someone used a warped bowl to guide the style.

The zombie probably saw her as one big delicious brain.

Aloha's eyes flitted to Elvis still on the kitchen side of the door. She mouthed for him to hurry. He nodded and finally came through the swinging door.

Since Hanson Braddock kept his restaurant in good repair the door had been oiled recently and made no noise when it eased open.

She thanked the heavens for small mercies.

Elvis held the net gun in both hands, the barrel pointed slightly down, his beady eyes narrow and focused on the grunting zombie. As the zombie shuffled toward Aloha, Elvis raised the gun and took aim. The net gun had a wide barrel like that of an oversized double-barreled shotgun, so it was not easy to raise the heavy weapon in order to fire it. The zombie would be unable to move.

No fuss. No muss.

After the thing was subdued they'd put it in the pen out back of the town hall where they kept the whacked-out zombies until a decision could be made about what to do with the undead. Elvis stepped to within the range recommended in the gun's user manual, then raised the gun and pulled the trigger. A loud click was followed by silence. Once Elvis pulled the trigger the net should have deployed to ensnare the zombie in a net big enough to envelope his entire body.

A dud? Oh. Oh. Wayta go, Dr. Oh! Aloha moved her feet, but they slipped out from under her, and suddenly she was airborne. She landed hard on her tail-bone, the shock traveling up her spine and forcing the air from her lungs. Spots danced before her now teary eyes, and she blinked at the sharp pain at the base of her spine. Her chest hurt as she struggled to take in a breath.

Man, that hurts.

Through hazy vision she saw the zombie shuffling closer and closer. Her nose wrinkled. He reeked of rotting garbage.

She tried to move, but her legs were too weak. She tried not to panic as she realized she was unable to move. She couldn't breathe, couldn't get her lungs to bring in any air.

In her oxygen-deprived mind it suddenly dawned on her what would happen next if she were unable to move.

Oh, crap, he's gonna eat my brain

The round glass light fixtures hanging from the diner's ceiling threw rainbows of brilliant color across the ceiling tiles. The echo of shuffling footsteps followed by a sharp grunt made her tense.

She was about to become the main course on the brain-only diet plan.

A swish, a snap, followed by a yelp of surprise, announced something dropped heavily next to her on the cool tile. In Aloha's foggy mind she sensed the human-shape had to be the hungry zombie. The smell of rotten fruit confirmed her realization.

Finally her aching lungs managed to draw in a sharp breath of air. She tried to speak. "What …" Her voice dropped to a hiss.

She cleared her throat and tried again, but no words came out. She was certain that if she looked up the definition of the word *frustration* her picture would be there.

"It's OK, Sheriff, don't try to talk." Hanson Braddock, he of the handsome, dimpled, tanned features came into view as her mind cleared. A loop of dark curls fell across his slightly wrinkled forehead above hazel eyes that brimmed with genuine concern.

She nodded and took in several deep breaths. The light-headedness slowly dissipated, and her faculties gradually returned.

Aloha sat upright, gasping for breathe since she landed on her tailbone. She wiggled her toes to help increase circulation and looked around to find the zombie lying face down on the tiled floor next to her with a rope securing its ankles. It lay unmoving, but seemed to be breathing, evidenced by the rise and fall of its back.

It was out. But it sure must've hit the floor hard. Aloha winced. *Ouch.*

"What happened?" She finally managed to croak. She coughed to clear her throat. She was relieved to find her throat felt better.

Hanson stood up, his lean, muscular frame sending shivers through Aloha. The restaurant's owner was all man and incredibly sexy. He grinned, deepening the dimples on his cheeks. His eyes sparkled. "I was a cowboy in my former life." He hooked his thumbs on the front pockets of his tight jeans. "I used to be pretty good with a rope."

"It seems you still are." Aloha held out one hand, and Hanson's warm hand engulfed hers as he helped her stand. Once on her feet she reluctantly released his hand. Man, was he strong.

"You two make a cute couple."

Aloha turned to glare at old man McDok still seated in the red leather booth. He grinned at them. It pleased her when he shriveled and dropped his eyes to his table under her disapproving gaze.

"You think so?" Hanson said, cheerily.

Aloha faced Hanson as her features relaxed. Her cheeks must've been as red as a slice of ripe watermelon.

"Hey, Sheriff." Elvis came up to them, the net gun loosely gripped in his huge fingers. "You OK?"

Relieved by the distraction Aloha snatched the net gun out of Elvis's hands before he could protest. "What's wrong with this thing?"

She scanned the gun's faux wood stock and immediately spotted the problem. Elvis had left the safety on.

"Elvis! My brain could have been eaten." She demonstrated the weapon's safety by flicking it off and on with her thumb.

The corners of the big man's eyes drooped, and he avoided her glare by looking at the zombie.

The zombie grunted as it woke from its dreamless sleep. At least she hoped for its sake it was dreamless.

She stole a glance at Hanson and thought she saw a flash of disapproval from him at the way she spoke to Elvis. "Oh, never mind. Why don't you take the zom to the holding area?" She raised a single eyebrow at him.

Elvis met her gaze as his expression brightened. He nodded, then leaned over and grabbed the zombie's right arm in his meaty fingers and pulled the creature to its feet. The zombie stood, its shoulders slumped, and emitted a low growl. The undead man pulled at Elvis's grip, trying to break loose.

Elvis's knuckles whitened as he tightened his hold. "We'll have none of that, zom. You better come along quietly if you know what's good for ya." The deputy patted the canister of zom-repellant spray on his belt; it was identical to the one Aloha had affixed to hers.

Aloha flinched. *Oh, man.* She forgot about the spray.

The zombie's expression changed to a mixture of fear and timid submission at sight of the canister, and he stopped pulling. Zombie's hated the new spray. Not that she blamed them.

A week previous, the town's major employer, the Totally Zip Corporation, had issued her and Elvis an experimental spray repellent designed to stop attacking zombies by freezing them like statues. In the sales pitch video she'd seen, the zombie test subject's eye movements indicated the undead creature's senses were still active after it was frozen. It knew it was helpless.

Aloha shuddered as she recalled the pitiful whimpering of the frozen test subject as it strained to move.

And the cry of pain when the lab technician broke the zom's left arm to demonstrate how helpless the undead subject had become under the spray's influence.

And how horrified she'd been when she read the instruction pamphlet, which stated that side effects to the subject included possible prolonged skin irritation, headache and vomiting, watery eyes and, in extreme cases, the subject's skin melting off to become a puddle of primordial goo.

Subject was such a dehumanizing term. Aloha preferred to think of the zoms as victims. After all, zombies had once been people too.

The pamphlet went on to assure the customer that death after using zom spray was extremely unlikely.

Yeah, right. Like when a building collapses on your head it's extremely unlikely you'll be crushed. Get real.

Hanson knelt down next to the zombie's feet and removed the lasso from round his ankles. "You need any help getting it to the corral, Deputy?"

"It's not an *it! It's* a person." Aloha spat her words indignantly, eliciting slack-jawed surprise from both Hanson and Elvis. Even the zombie looked startled by the fierceness of her reaction. Aloha immediately chastised herself for snapping at them. Too often she thought of them as *it*s, and since her ex-boyfriend had once been a half zombie the subject was a trigger for her temper.

Aloha cheeks again grew warm. She lowered her voice, "Huh, sorry. I meant to say zombies are people first and brain-munching monsters second."

Elvis and Hanson looked at each other, then shrugged in unison.

Aloha looked at her Timex. "I've gotta go. I'm late for my meeting with the mayor."

Not waiting for a response, she spun around intending to make a dignified exit but slipping on the tiles and waving her arms about like a mad chicken instead.

Finally, she managed to stumble out the door to the sidewalk and took in a deep breath. Immediately dizziness gripped her.

Car horns and the rush of tires on pavement from the traffic sounded louder than normal. Her heart was still racing, and her forehead was dotted with beads of sweat. *What's wrong with me?* She'd been a L.I.P.S. agent for six years and been in more tight scrapes and near-death experiences than she could count. Of course, the enemy agents, mad scientists, and super villains she'd encountered only wanted to kill her, not eat her. A shiver ran down her spine. The undead were creepy.

A sudden burst on an air horn made her look to her left in time to see the wide chrome grill of a large delivery truck careening toward her.

Through the windshield of the truck, she could see the driver's panicky face and wide eyes as she tried but failed to regain control of her truck. The air brakes locked, followed by the hiss of the air bleeding out. The smell of burning rubber permeated the air as the truck's tires laid a strip of black rubber straight toward where her VW Beetle patrol car sat parked at the curb.

Aloha realized when the truck rear-ended her sheriff's car it would drive the small car over the sidewalk right into where she now stood. And she knew she would have no time to react.

Why did this remind her of the old joke about the last thing that goes through a fly's mind when it hits a windshield?

Geez, I hope my butt doesn't taste funny.

She closed her eyes and cringed as she heard a loud *bang* followed by the screech of metal on metal.

Chapter Two

JOE'S FAMILY DINER'S TOP WAITRESS, Betty Strongbow, had returned to work after the zombie incident and was standing at the other end of the counter, making a fresh pot of coffee.

"Hey, Betty," Hanson said casually.

She looked up from the coffee pot. Her gray eyes were curious.

"I'm going out. I shouldn't be long." *I hope.*

Before Hanson could untie his apron, he heard a louder screech of brakes from the street. He reacted out of pure instinct and raced out the door in time to see a delivery truck about to run into the rear of the sheriff's bug patrol car.

He clearly saw the patrol car would be shoved up onto the sidewalk and into Aloha. She would be killed for sure.

The ear-splitting screech of metal striking metal affected him like a bell would a prizefighter. He leaped into action and covered the distance between himself and Aloha faster than he'd ever moved in his life.

He tackled her football-style, his arms wrapped around her slender waist. She grunted in surprise. Locked together, they flew across the cement just as the Beetle filled the spot where she'd been standing.

The car slammed into the side of the red brick bank building next to the diner with a sharp bang and a crunch of metal as the bumper absorbed the impact. The Beetle's front window cracked in a spider-web pattern.

Lying on top of Aloha, Hanson marveled that a mound of broken bricks where the wall of the zombie repair shop next to his restaurant used to be now covered the car's crumpled front end. He was breathing hard, and his heart still beat rapidly in his chest. The car was so a write-off. *The sheriff's not going to like it.*

He rolled off her and realized her head had hit the cement sidewalk. She was unconscious but still breathing.

Oh, oh. I think I hurt her.

He looked around and spotted the deputy standing beside his tricked-out pickup truck with the zom from the diner. He looked, wide-eyed, at the shattered Beetle in the wall. "Hey, Elvis! A little help here."

~~~

After the ambulance left to take Aloha to the hospital, and ensuring she was going to be OK, Hanson returned to the diner and now stood behind the counter, leaning his weight on a broom handle. He'd washed the floor only this morning, but the scuffle with the zombie had left behind patches of dead flesh. As he swept, a small pile of gray skin began to form in front of the broom's bristles.

Zoms sure are messy. He was glad now he had bought Joe's place rather than one of the zombie-only diners in town. He'd probably be seeing more of Sheriff Armstrong in the future. At least he hoped so. Having the local sheriff's department as customers was a diner's bread and butter.

Sure, Aloha Armstrong seemed like a bit of a stuffed shirt sometimes, but there was something about her he liked — something besides her tight uniform. And he wasn't about to let her die on the street. His father raised him to help others.

Aloha surprised him; she seemed tough and no-nonsense. *I like that in a woman.*

It impressed him. Aloha wasn't able to demonstrate how well she could handle herself with that out-of-control zom, but he sensed she had skills he hadn't seen yet. The air of confidence surrounding her was intoxicating.

Hanson had been in Zomopolis for only a few months and had already learned that loose lips led to uncomfortable questions about why he came to town and where he was from. He wasn't about to reveal his real reason for being in Zomopolis until he had solid evidence. Only then he'd tell Aloha what he was doing.

But his plan was coming together nicely. So far he'd spoken to about half the town's human residents.

"I still think you make a cute couple," said Albert with a suggestive wink.

Hanson looked up from the pile of gray skin in front of the broom, not realizing he'd been so lost in thought. Albert McDok had sat in the booth all morning just as he did every morning. If this were a bar they'd call him a barfly, but Hanson had taken a liking to the old man. Besides he sometimes offered him some pretty valuable advice. "Hey, Mr. McDok," Hanson smiled thinly. "What was that?" He asked as if he hadn't heard the old man.

"I said you and the new sheriff make a cute couple."

Hanson's cheeks grew warm. "I don't even know her."

McDok chuckled. "What's that got to do with the price of pie?

I chased the late Mrs. McDok halfway cross the country before she agreed to marry me, and it isn't like I saved her life like you did the sheriff's."

Hanson's face felt warm. He nodded, his eyes focused on the broom's bristles as he swept. "So you stalked her?"

Mr. McDok snorted. "We called it *courting* in my day."

Hanson liked old man McDok. Everyone seemed to think he was a perv, but he was actually very wise. He'd suggested a new coffee supplier for the shop, which saved Hanson a lot of overhead money.

Hanson stopping sweeping and set his chin on the broom handle, both hands gripping the shaft. "All right, since you're such an expert, what should I do?"

"Do what Russell Crowe or Mel Gibson would do — go after her."

"Right now?"

McDok shook his head. "And you're waiting for what, exactly?"

Hanson leaned the broom against the counter. *McDok's right.* Getting to know the sheriff better would help him find out what she knew. If he befriended her, and she found any evidence, maybe she'd tell him what she'd discovered before anyone else.

Chapter Three

ALOHA OPENED HER EYES and winced. Her head pounded so hard it seemed about to split in half. She blinked repeatedly until her vision cleared and she could take in her surroundings.

Her whole body ached. Even her eyeballs hurt.

She half-expected to see a puffy cloud with an angel sitting on it, but instead she saw walls painted a shade of pale yellow and a faux oak table beside the hospital bed she lay on. Thick beige drapes covered the single window, so she had no idea if it was night or day.

A smiling man with a dark complexion entered the room. He wore a knee-length white lab coat, a powder-blue shirt, and tan slacks. The echo of footsteps in the hallway outside followed the door swinging closed behind him. A stethoscope hung round his neck and down the front of his shirt. It swung back and forth in time to his movements. "Hello, Sheriff."

Aloha hung her head and scrunched into a ball as she planted her hands over her ears. "Hey!" she scolded in a hoarse whisper, "don't shout!"

The man's smile disappeared. His brow creased. "Sorry," he whispered.

He stood at the foot of the bed and picked up the medical chart hanging off a hook attached to the footboard.

Aloha dropped her hands from her ears, sank into the soft pillow behind her, and sighed. That was better.

The man scanned the chart, then placed it back on the hook and buried his hands in the pockets of his lab coat. His eyes were serious as he studied her.

He didn't say anything for several minutes, which made her think he had bad news for her. She forced herself not to squirm under his steady gaze.

Finally, he cleared his throat, and the smile came back over his angular features. "You're going to be fine, Sheriff. You had a nasty fall, but the x-rays don't show a concussion. Just minor bruising and a few cuts and scrapes. Nothing serious."

"Are you the doctor?"

The man suddenly burst out laughing, making her head pound. He held out one hand and winced. His voice dropped to a whisper again. "Of course, sorry. I forget sometimes when patients arrive unconscious they may not know who I am."

She shook his offered hand. His flesh was warm and firm, reassuring. "I'm Dr. Kupta. I don't believe we've met. I'm the town doctor."

The corner of her mouth curled up slightly. Even this tiny movement elicited a shot of pain behind her eyes. Her lips puckered like she'd sucked on a lemon.

Dr. Kupta released her hand and stuffed his back into the pocket of his lab coat. "The pain will subside. I've given you your maximum daily dosage of pain killer, so I'm sorry, but you'll have to wait for until tomorrow for more."

"Tomorrow? I can't stand another minute." She had closed her eyes but now opened them to see the grin on Kupta's dusky features.

He used the index finger of his left hand to push his wire-framed glasses up his wide nose. She noted the wedding band on the ring finger of his left hand.

"Married?" she asked, changing the subject, anything to distract herself from the pain.

He smiled easily. "Why, yes, how did you know?"

Normally she would have nodded, but she lifted her right arm and pointed to the gold band. "The ring."

He chuckled. "Oh, yes, of course, I almost forgot; cops have built in married-guy detectors, don't they? Especially when they're wearing a ring on THE finger." He punctuated his joke with a laugh.

She smiled and realized she liked this man. He seemed honest and warm. Good traits for a small-town doctor, and with only 1,313 residents, Zomopolis certainly qualified for the small-town designation. And he was funny. Any man with a well-developed sense of humor was OK by her.

She'd only been in Zomopolis for a week and already had almost been dinner for a brain-eating zombie and was nearly run over by a delivery truck. What else was going to happen?

Her brow wrinkled. *I recall a truck coming at my...* "My car. What happened to my patrol car? Is the driver OK?"

Kupta nodded. "The driver's fine, but I'm told your car is totaled. But you better ask your deputy. He called twenty minutes ago saying he's on his way here."

"Actually, where is *here*?"

Kupta chuckled, and the corners of his eyes wrinkled slightly. "You know where the community center is on Ukulele Street, right?"

Without thinking she nodded. This time there was no pain. *Cool, I'm getting better already.*

"We're behind the center."

"How did I get here?"

He smiled and rocked back on his heels. "You're in our humble but well-meaning hospital. I also drive the ambulance."

"A one-man band, huh?"

He nodded.

The door to the hallway opened, interrupting them, and she heard Elvis's baritone voice say, "Thank you, ma'am. Thank you very much."

She wanted to roll her eyes but didn't for fear of the pain it might cause. *Oh, brother, is he a hambone or what?* The guy was the worst Elvis impersonator ever.

Unlike his namesake, Deputy Elvis Bushwood preferred rap music.

Elvis stood before her, unshaven, a little out of breath, and his uniform so badly wrinkled and dirty she thought at first he'd been in a fight. She made a mental note to write him up for being in such a disheveled condition in public. "We have the obligation to look and act professionally at all times when on duty," she'd told him on her first day on the job. He'd said he understood; now in only a week he'd gone all native on her.

"Uh, hi, Sheriff." Elvis offered her a weak smile and then shifted his gaze to the doctor. "Doc, can you give us a minute?"

He nodded. "Certainly, Deputy." He swung his gaze to Aloha. "My nurse will be in later to check on you, Sheriff. For now, please get some rest. No matter what emergency arises I want you to stay in bed and rest." The doctor regarded Elvis with a blank expression on his face.

Aloha grinned. "Ok, Doctor. No worries."

After Dr. Kupta had left the room Elvis explained where he'd been and what had happened in his usual rapid-fire style.

Though she'd only met him a week ago he seemed like an old hound that lay on the porch in the sun scratching himself until something interesting happened. She pushed away the image of Elvis scratching himself.

"Sheriff. We have a problem. A *big* problem."

"Elvis," Aloha said, "first, please, whisper. Second, slow down and tell me what's going on, and, third, tell me about my car." She'd only had the car for a week but already she'd come to love the little Beetle with its roomy interior and peppy engine.

Elvis looked from one side of the room to the other, and then leaned closer. He smelled like eau de chilidog. At least he whispered this time. "Sorry. Bugs?"

What's the use? Why fight it? She nodded.

He continued, "Thought so. Zomopolis is crawlin' with 'em. But the wall is comin' down." He held up his left hand and displayed three fingers. He lowered one finger. "Your car is totaled." He lowered another finger, leaving a single digit in the middle of his fist. He frowned, and his eyes narrowed. "Is that three or two?" He stared at the lone finger, his frown deepening.

She didn't believe it. He was giving her the finger.

She placed a hand over his single finger and lowered it. She smiled at him. "Don't worry about the number, Big E. Just tell me about the wall. What wall, and why is it coming down?"

"It's the dome's fourth wall, Sheriff. Billy Buick called the office and told me he and the crew repaired a tear in the dome wall yesterday, and when they went back to check it today they found not only is the tear back but it's larger than ever."

Aloha dropped her arms to her sides on top of the white sheets. Her forehead wrinkled as she considered Elvis's words. *Larger?* How was that possible?

The fourth wall had kept the zombies confined in Zomopolis for over forty years. If Elvis was right, this was very bad news. If the zoms escaped they'd invade the world and eat every brain in sight.

She had been in worse spots, but they had better go check out the break in the dome wall. One could never tell how bad the situation unless one saw it in person. "Did I get a new car?"

Elvis immediately shifted his gaze from her to the floor, and his tanned face suddenly had a distinctive reddish hue.

"Tell me," she said softly.

He looked back at her as his broad shoulders slumped in resignation. "It's in the hospital parking lot." He shook his head, and his eyes drooped at the corners. "But you're not gonna like it."

One side of Aloha's mouth curled up. The zoms escaping was bad, a new car that made her look ridiculous as the new sheriff of America's only zombie haven meant to keep the country safe from undead brain-munches, how terrible could it be? "Oh, come now, Big E, it can't be that bad."

~~~

Aloha's headache pounded out Beethoven's Fifth Symphony inside her head, cannons and all. She stared at the car the town had replaced her Beetle with. Her legs trembled, but she managed to stay standing.

Some patrol car. And she thought her old patrol car was small. This car made the VW look like a limousine. The thing was smaller than the bathroom in her bachelorette apartment.

"What is it?"

"Huh, the mayor says it's called a *Huvo*. It's a prototype electric car. The mayor buys electric car prototypes to save the town money and to go green." Elvis stepped up and opened a flap at the back of the one-seat car. "You plug it in."

Zombies, eat me now. "But my Beetle isn't — I mean, wasn't — a prototype."

Elvis fell silent; his too-big-to-be-normal shoes shuffling back and forth like those of a child who'd been caught with his hand in the cookie jar.

She glared at him, and her forehead wrinkled. "It's not, right?"

"Well ... not exactly," he began.

"Out with it, big man, or you'll be the last deputy Zomopolis will ever have."

"Yeah. I know." He took in a deep breath and then exhaled nosily. "The Beetle had a nuclear-powered engine. The company that modified it went out of business because of rumors of leaky reactor shields and," he hesitated, "side effects."

Aloha's eyes went wide. "Leaky shields? You mean I'm going to glow in the dark?"

Elvis shook his head vigorously. "Oh, no, no, Sheriff. The mayor would never give you a dangerous car." His line of sight dropped to the pavement again to avoid her quizzical glare.

His poker face was terrible.

"Do you play poker?"

He glanced up at her. "Yeah. Why?"

The corners of her mouth curled in a brief smile. "Let me know next time you have a game. I'd *love* to sit in."

And win your weight in cash, she thought.

Aloha walked around the strange, egg-shaped vehicle. She'd never seen anything remotely like this car before.

The front was comprised of mostly Plexiglas, and the steering wheel reminded her of an old-fashioned airplane wheel she'd seen in old Tom Cruise movies.

Tom Cruise movies were so cool. Too bad he never appeared in any incarnation of her favorite television show when she was a child: *Star Trek The Next Generation*. She always wondered why. That show was epic. Captain Picard...so sexy. A shiver ran up her spine at the recollection of his baldhead and deep, bedroom voice.

She shook off the image; instead shifting her concentration to the tiny car (there was a sticker on the windshield she had to peer at closely in order to read) had no room for more than her. She doubted she'd be able to close the door while wearing her sidearm. And would she be able to participate in a high-speed chase in this thing? She wondered what she'd do if she arrested someone. Maybe there was a roof-rack accessory?

She frowned. Does Zomopolis even have car chases?

"By the way, a package came for you from some guy named Oh? I put it in the trunk for you," Elvis said.

Aloha's only reply was a nod. No doubt the doc had provided her another of his new non-lethal inventions for this assignment. She'd look at it later.

As far as she could tell from her review of the files on her first few days, the worst thing that had ever happened since the town was founded, long before she was born in 1979, involved an old lady who died of a heart attack while climbing a tree. That happened in 1991 when Mrs. Wilson tried to rescue her cat, Busstop, who was stuck up a tree on Obo Street.

The town's residents may have included many walking undead but crime was virtually non-existent.

Aloha looked at Elvis. He shuffled his feet more furiously, as if the urge to pee was about to win the day. "You OK?"

He nodded, but his cheeks were flushed. Finally he shook his head. "Huh, sorry, but I've really gotta get out to where the wall repair team is working."

"Why so urgent? Are the zom's getting loose?" He shook his head. Thank goodness, she thought.

"My brother's out there, and I —"

"It's a lot worse than you alluded to, isn't it?"

He looked at her like she'd suddenly grown two heads, which in this town was a definite possibility. Aloha grunted. "Sorry, you told me there is a problem with the wall the crew was repairing?"

"Not exactly. More like someone got sucked through the tear in the wall."

Her brow wrinkled. "Yeah, that's pretty serious."

A single tear slipped from Elvis's left eye and rolled down his puffy cheek to drip off the end of his dimpled chin. "My little brother, Jerry Lee Bushwood, got sucked through the dome wall into the fourth dimension."

Oh, crap, thought Aloha as her body went cold, *it actually is worse than I thought. People are getting sucked into another dimension?* She placed a comforting hand *on* Elvis' shoulder but her concern went far beyond him and his brother. If the zombies got loose... *I hope this isn't the beginning of the end of the world, as we know it.*

Chapter Four

ELVIS TURNED LEFT ON UKULELE STREET from the hospital parking lot, and the truck's engine roared as it increased speed. When she first saw the tiny medical building, which doubled as the pet clinic, Aloha wondered if calling it a hospital was an exaggeration. Now that she'd been a patient she decided it was.

The part time nurse, who she discovered was Dr. Kupta's wife, Desirée, insisted Aloha not leave the hospital until she was fully recovered. But Aloha told her she had urgent police business to attned to without explaining the problem with the fourth wall. No reason to start a panic.

For Aloha, though, the chance for a little action not directed at her made the adrenaline surge in her veins. Her pain forgotten, she'd climbed into the passenger seat of Elvis's four-wheel drive pickup and buckled herself in faster than she'd done in a long time. Action was what she lived for.

Danger was her middle name. Her real middle name was Wikiwiki, but danger sounded cooler for a secret agent.

As soon as they were headed south on Ukelele Street, speeding past the rows of three bedroom bungalows, Elvis flipped on the lights and siren.

On the elm-lined street, children rode bicycles on the sidewalks while men and women cut their lawns and weeded flower beds as they watched the truck roar by.

Aloha chuckled with glee, rolled down the window, and rested her arm on the doorframe. The wind blew her long Titian red hair behind her and felt amazing on her skin. She loved the sensation.

It surprised her when the siren came on because it made that hee-haw sound reminiscent of English police cars. Now that was certainly different thna she was used to. *Must be an import.*

Wow! Cool!

She knew the sound well because she'd spent three years working undercover in England to stop a supervillian named Nicky Pepperoni from blowing up the Houses of Parliament. Pepperoni managed to slip away before she could arrest him, but what did people expect when the villian was named after a greasy sausage?

She did manage to defuse the bomb with the bomb-detector-deactivator-and-vegetable-slicer Dr. Oh supplied her with from his weapons lab. Thing made a pretty good julienne carrot too. She always wondered why Dr. Oh didn't do infomercials. He could have made a fortune selling his gadgets for home use.

The police in England preferred a very distinctive siren over the wailer commonly used in America.

She leaned left as the truck fishtailed when they rounded the corner at the intersection of Trumpet and Flute. The few cars and trucks at the intersection stopped at the sight of the truck with its flashing roof light bar and strange wheezing siren.

She saw a woman with jet-black hair staring wide-eyed at them as they sped past her. Aloha chuckled to herself.

They must look like the strangest pair of cops ever. Her, with her too-tight uniform, and a bald man-mountain driving his truck like a maniac.

She held her breath as they skidded up onto two wheels around another corner. They were now headed west on the Violin Highway, tipped to one side at a forty-five degree angle, balanced on only two wheels.

The truck slammed down hard onto all four wheels again and fishtailed until Elvis managed to regain control. Aloha was tossed hard against the seatbelt straps. "Whoa! Slow down, Big E!"

She tested the spot with her fingertips where the seatbelt strap had dug into her flesh through her shirt. She winced. It hurt.

That's gonna leave a bruise.

Elvis's soft brown eyes were narrowed to slits in concentration, and beads of sweat dotted across his wide, wrinkled forehead and ran down his face in rivulets. He wasn't listening to her anymore. His knuckles were white from gripping the steeringwheel too tightly. His broad shoulders slumped forward as his eyes focused on the road ahead. The truck weaved around slower vehicles.

Aloha's eyes flitted to the speedometer. The needle was buried at the right end of the dial. The cabin rattled around her as if the truck was about to shake itself apart any second.

Whew! It was at times like this she was glad she learned to buckle-up-for-safety when she was a kid.

If she remembered correctly, the highway led to a gate. After the gate, you drove through a mile-long tunnel that ended next to an orchard. An energy barrier surrounded the perimeter, encompassing the entire town and keeping the zombies inside and would-be intruders outside.

Rumors were that beyond the fourth wall was another dimension. Aloha had seen a lot of strange things on her L.I.P.S. missions but nothing had made her think there was another dimension beyond the wall. An alligator-filled swamp, sure, but another plane of existence? What nonsense. She snorted. *Urban myths are total crap.*

In 1969 the government had set up Zomopolis as a research project to study how and why zombies were created and to find a cure. Except for the support services, most of the town's residents had doctorates in biochemistry, mythology, nucleur science and medicine, radiology, and other related sciences.

Aloha's job, she'd complained, was to babysit a bunch of eccentric scientists.

A few of the town's residents stayed even after retirement. Mr. McDok, for one. He'd been one of the original researchers brought to Zomopolis to unravel the problem of zombies.

These people scared her the most. Why would any sane person voluntarily stay in the town where half the residents were undead?

It seemed a little creepy to her.

When Zombie Away was discovered it cured ninety percent of zombies, making them human again. Unfortunately, the other ten percent were either allergic or the cure didn't work.

The background mission briefing materials provided by L.I.P.S. contained reports that provided theories about why Zombie Away didn't have a 100 percent cure rate as advertised. Lots of theories but no consensus.

While Aloha didn't fully understand all the scientists said in these reports, it was clear they could not even agree on the root cause of what caused zombies, or any foolproof way to change zombified victims back to humans (the emphasis on *fool*).

The bottom line was: Zomopolis had 202 zombie residents and 309 human residents. Some zombies were created by magic, others by chemicals, including chemical accidents. Whenever she spilled anything, Aloha worried she'd just created a new zombie somewhere in the world.

"Here we are," Elvis muttered.

Finally, the wall of the dome, painted-sky-blue to mimic real sky, came into view.

At the edge of long rows of fruit trees heavy with apples and pears, three trucks marked the site of the work crew. Each white truck wore its familiar red triangle logo on its doors. The center of each triangle bore the familiar font of THE FOURTH WALL 2 LIVE CREW with the company motto of *We Serve to Save You and Your Brain* in smaller type below. A group of five workmen in coveralls stood in a small knot in front of the trucks. They looked up when Elvis stomped on the brake, sending the pickup swerving and fishtailing as it skid across the pavement. It headed toward them like an unsteady missile of steel and glass.

The sound of screeching tires on pavement split the air, and the odor of burning rubber filled the truck's interior. Aloha had one hand on the dashboard in front of her, the other gripping the doorframe. *Oh, crap!* Her heart beat faster with each passing second, and her eyes bulged.

It looked like they weren't going to stop in time and would crash into into one of the work trucks. The group of workers yelled angrily and scattered like pins in a bowling alley before the rampaging example of Detroit engineering.

Aloha closed her eyes tight and held her breath.

Finally the truck came to a bone-jarring stop, and she was thrown forward hard against the seatbelt.

"Owww! Elvis! You idiot! That really hurts!"

Inside, Aloha was relieved when she didn't hear metal on metal.

She opened one eye and saw the work truck over the hood of the pickup. It was close, too close.

She released the breath she'd been holding in with a *whoosh*.

Elvis threw open the driver's door and was out of the truck cab before she could stop him. She marveled that the pickup's steering wheel was bent and misshapen.

Man, is he one strong dude. Good to know-for-the-future-file information about her deputy.

After a struggle with the release mechanism holding her seatbelt in place, Aloha cut the strap with her utility knife, opened the passenger door, and stepped out. Walking around to the front of the pickup she saw that the bumpers of the two trucks were actually touching.

She shook her head, then looked for Elvis. She spotted him standing glaring down at a short, gray-haired man with black framed glasses perched on the tip of his hawk-like nose. The deputy towered over the man like the giant at the top of the beanstalk. While she couldn't make out what they were saying, Elvis was waving his arms about and his face was flushed. His voice grew louder and louder with each passing second.

Suddenly Elvis pulled his gun from its holster and took a step toward the small man who stood his ground seemingly unfazed by this large, gun-waving, red-faced deputy coming at him.

Aloha broke into a run. She had to stop him before he hurt someone.

Her heart pounding in her ears, her breathing rapid, she rushed head down at the two men. As she ran she heard Elvis shout, "I'm gonna kill you!" just before a shot rang out.

"Very funny, Elvis." The smaller man shook his head with an expression of disgust on his ruddy features. His brown eyes peered over his glasses at Elvis, who stood in front of him breathing hard, the smoking gun now hanging loosely at his hip, the barrel pointing at the ground.

Aloha came up beside her deputy and snatched his service automatic out of his hand. He glanced at her, shrugged, then turned back to look at the small man. An oval-shaped, white cloth patch stitched over the left breast of the man's gray coveralls identified him as *CHIEF* in styled red letters. This meant he must be the boss.

Aloha looked up at the protective dome's fake sky far above and hoped the bullet hadn't made a hole up there when Elvis fired the 9mm Glock over his head. She glared into Elvis's eyes and shook her head slightly.

The anger in his eyes dissipated under her gaze, and he shrugged slightly. She nodded. He understood she was upset with him and that they'd have a serious talk about this later.

She dropped her gaze to the other man. This had to be Billy Buick. Aloha stuck out her right hand in greeting. "Hi, Mr. Buick. I'm Aloha Armstrong, the new sheriff of Zomopolis."

Billy shifted his gaze to her, then took her hand in his. He shook her hand once, then released it. His forehead wrinkled as he looked her up and down. "Uniform's a little tight, don't you think?"

She cringed inside but forced a smile to her lips. "Yes, but I hear there's been some trouble, which is why I'm here." She glanced at Elvis, whose shoulders had slumped as he gazed hang-dog-like at the ground. "I mean why *we're* here."

Billy chuckled dryly. "That may be why you're here, Sheriff, but Elvis is looking for his brother. I've known these boys since they was kids. They've always been close as two brothers can be."

He turned and headed away toward another truck parked off to the right of where Elvis's pickup sat.

In the passenger seat of Billy's truck sat a large bloodhound who stared at them with sad eyes and droopy ears.

Using her index finger she signaled for Elvis to follow her behind his truck. His shoulders slumped, and he avoided her steady gaze. "What have you been doing? Were you really going to kill someone?"

He shook his head. "No way, Sheriff, I was just trying to scare him."

She nodded. "Well, we got bigger things to deal with right now, but later we're going to have a long talk about the safe use of firearms. OK?"

"Yes, ma'am," he said between gritted teeth. His face was flushed, and she could almost feel the anger emanating from him.

They rejoined the group just in time to see Billy Buick leaving. He called to them over his shoulder without looking back. "Daisy and me gotta go ta the TZC Labs research facility, but one of my guys will show ya around."

Billy hurried around the front of his work truck, got in, and sped off, leaving them and the rest of the work crew, and a clearly still very upset Elvis Bushwood, behind.

Aloha studied the work crew. Two men and two women. Aloha would never have mistaken them for people who worked with their hands. They looked a little too *Hollywood* for her liking, and she'd had enough of Hollywood types during her last L.I.P.S. case on a television reality show.

All four workmen (*workpeople?* she wondered) were dressed in blue jeans, tan work boots, and blue-and-gray checkered workshirts that hung loosely over the waist of their jeans.

The two men had similar height and build, had dark curly hair, dark eyes, and dark stubble on their rugged faces. They could have been twins they looked so much alike. But one had a jagged scar that ran down his left cheek from beside his left eye to nearly the tip of his chin.

In contrast, the two women were very different.

One was a willowy blonde about five-nine who would have rivaled one of the models walking the catwalks in Paris or New York. The other woman was shorter (Aloha estimated five-three) with auburn hair, a round face, and expressive hazel eyes. She smiled warmly as their eyes locked.

The brunette pulled off her heavy work gloves and walked toward Aloha, her bare hand extended. Aloha took it in hers and found the woman's skin surprisingly soft and not as rough as she would have thought.

"Hi, Sheriff. I'm Annie Oakley. I'm the forewoman."

Oh, Aloha thought, *Buick is the chief but she's in charge of the crew? Interesting. Nice Arkansas accent, but Annie Oakley? Has to be a fake name.* "Annie Oakley?"

Annie laughed, slapped her hands together, then covered her mouth with one hand, but Aloha sensed this animation was entirely a put on. *When will I learn to make friends without insulting them first*, she thought.

"You're new to town, right?" Annie said crossing her arms over her chest, and her now serious eyes regarded Aloha as her mouth formed a thin line. "We don't make fun of people around here, but seein' as you're new I'm gonna cut you some slack."

Annie turned away and nodded at the two men and the woman on her crew who nodded in kind then disappeared to the rear of the two trucks.

Aloha glanced at Elvis hoping to get an explanation for what just happened. He shrugged and winced as if in pain.

She decided he wasn't going to be any help at all. She had to learn to be careful what she said around here. This was one overly sensitive town.

Aloha reached into the bed of Elvis's truck and pulled out a leather bag in which she kept her running shoes. Ever since her second day on the job when she and Elvis responded to a call at Mrs. Scutter's house she'd kept a pair of running shoes stashed in every vehicle in the department just in case she had to run. Running in these clunky cop boots just didn't work for her, they were hardly stylish runner's wear.

Annie started to walk away. "Come with me. I'll show you where Jerry Lee disappeared."

"Uhh, OK, thanks." Aloha walked to stand beside Elvis and grabbed his thick arm in her fingers and squeezed hard. "You're coming with me, Big E," she whispered.

He nodded, and she released his arm. He rubbed his arm, then followed her to where Annie and her crew were suiting up in white protective suits.

Aloha looked around and didn't see additional suits for her and Elvis. "Huh, Ms. Oakley, what about us?"

Annie glanced up from pulling up the zipper on the front of her suit. "You won't be getting as close as we will. You should be fine." She looked away and spoke in low tones to her crew.

The one man Aloha had dubbed scarface looked at her briefly, chuckled grimly, then went back to retrieve a backpack on the tailgate of one of the work trucks.

Should be? Aloha mouthed to Elvis.

He nodded, then whispered. "They're supposed to be the best."

"We *are* the best," Annie interrupted, a hard edge to her voice.

Aloha looked at Annie, who was now dressed in a full-body protective suit, the only uncovered spot being her round face. She wore a backpack, which Aloha knew contained an air tank and a mask that would cover the wearer's face. Over the right breast of the suit was the same triangle logo as on the side of the work trucks, with the addition of a number above the tip of the triangle.

"Yes, Ms. Oakley, I'm sure you are the best." And Aloha meant every word. "Now, where are we going?"

A brief smile passed over Annie's lips, and her eyes narrowed. "Why, where no zombie has gone before, of course."

~~~

The moment they entered the orchard, the breeze picked up. The branches, heavy with fruit, swayed and swung at Aloha's head. She ducked as a thick apple tree branch nearly hit her before she managed to fend it off with one hand.

Glancing at Elvis, she saw he had his arms up with his elbows extended on both sides of his square head. He had the perfect system of guarding his face like a boxer until a sudden gust of wind made a branch thrust up between his arms and smack him in the chin, knocking him backward.

Aloha smiled to herself as big E shook off the sudden attack, then continued forward deeper into the orchard.

The crew around them had no trouble maneuvering through the trees and easily sidestepping the waving branches.

Aloha smelled something odd yet familiar in the air. She sniffed and thought she detected bubble gum. It was growing stronger the deeper they went into the trees.

She looked up and saw the curve of the dome wall was becoming more distinct with each passing minute.

She caught up with Annie. "How much farther?"

"Not far. We should see the scaffold beyond that next stand of trees."

Aloha followed Annie's line of sight and sure enough saw gray steel pipes through the trees.

Finally they stepped clear of the fruit trees into a grassy field that ran from the edge of the forest to the dome wall. White plastic boxes with the words INTER-DIMENSIONAL PATCHING COMPOUND stenciled on the side lay scattered around the base of the scaffold. The scaffold was anchored by steel cables embedded in the grass. The wood and steel frame rose twenty feet up the curved wall of the dome. Wooden planks for workers to stand on were supported on steel hooks set across horizontal bars at the four- and six-foot levels.

Aloha approached the scaffolding and craned her neck back as her gaze followed the curve of wall upward. And the curve of the dome was more pronounced standing here. She had to stop herself from falling backward when she scanned up seemingly toward infinity.

Whoa, this is one big mama.

Elvis appeared at her side, breathing hard. "Man, Sheriff that's some orchard."

"It's *orchid*, Big E, not orchard. An orchid is a flower."

Elvis snorted. "Yeah, I know. I'm not stupid, ya know. I meant orchid." He pointed to his right. "Over there."

Aloha looked around her deputy's bulk, and her jaw dropped. *Oh, boy.* He was right. That was some orchid.

Farther down the field stood a white and canary-yellow orchid that she estimated stood forty feet high. It was something right out of a fairy tale or some cheesy, direct-to-video science fiction movie.

"How?" She paused, and a frown wrinkled her brow. "Why?"

She shook her head. That wasn't right. "Who?" She fell silent again. She was fresh out of Ws.

"I can explain." A familiar male voice from behind her made her look over her shoulder. Her jaw dropped again.

Today was full of surprises. One thing about this job was it certainly wasn't going to be boring. Her day had just turned handsome.

Cafe owner Hanson Braddock, wearing a sleeveless white shirt and blue jeans, stepped from the stand of fruit trees into the clearing. Most surprising was the two-headed axe he held in his strong hands and the look of pure anger on his chiseled features.

Chapter Five

ELVIS HITCHED UP HIS GUN belt, lowered his head, and marched toward Hanson. "Hold it right there, Mr. Braddock."

"Get out of my way, Elvis. I'm going to knock it down." He flexed his arms, causing his biceps to ripple and the muscles on his forearms to tense.

Surprisingly, Elvis shook his head. His eyes narrowed as his full lips formed a grim line of determination. Like a cop directing traffic at an intersection, he held out one hand, the other gripping the butt of the pistol in his holster. The two men came at each other like they were entering the epicenter of the perfect storm.

She had to do something or this was going to end badly.

Aloha rushed to stand between them with her arms held out, her palms up. She glared first at Elvis, then at Hanson. They didn't appear about to slow down.

"Stop!" She braced her legs by spreading them wide and locking her knees.

She let out her breath as the men came to a halt, staring at each other, anger flushing their cheeks. Both men were breathing hard.

"Good. Now tell me what's going on?"

A snort of derision from Annie made Aloha look in the forewoman's direction.

She stood with her arms crossed; one corner of her mouth curled upward in obvious amusement.

"What's so funny?" Aloha lowered her arms to her sides.

Annie chuckled. "It's rare to see two boys scrapping over a giant orchid. Kinda surreal, don't ya think?"

"The orchid? I don't understand." Aloha was sick of not understanding.

"Yes!" Hanson pointed at the giant orchid. "That *thing* is going to kill us all. Someone has to stop it." He turned and began to swing the axe over his head, yelling like an ancient warrior going into battle.

Without thinking, Aloha ran after him, uncertain what exactly she would do if she caught up with the crazed cafe owner. She looked up at the orchid and wondered how such a beautiful, delicate plant could be a threat to anyone. Hanson's mailing address must've been in Paranoiaville.

When she closed the distance between herself and Hanson she leapt forward into the air and wrapped her arms around his legs and shoved him forward. He grunted as she tackled him from behind. She held on as the momentum carried him face-first onto the grass. Four older brothers had come in handy on more than one occasion.

They struck the ground hard, and the air rushed from Aloha's lungs. Her bruised body shocked her with searing pain like an electric current up and down her frame. She gritted her teeth. *That hurt. Not smart.*

Elvis arrived to stand over her. She heard the ratchet sounds of handcuffs. "You can let go, Sheriff. I got 'im."

Aloha let go of Hanson's legs, then rolled onto her back. Her breath came in gasps, and red, yellow, and green spots danced across her field of vision.

Elvis's massive head reappeared over her, only he was upside down. The shape of his tooth-missing grin reminded her of a Halloween pumpkin.

Perfect imagery for this town.

His dark eyes were quizzical, and a frown creased his wide forehead. "You OK?"

She nodded and sat up, her arms behind her on the soft grass to prop her up. She coughed twice as oxygen surged through her bloodstream.

"What is this all about?" she said, her voice raspy in her ears.

"He was gonna cut down my orchid."

Aloha turned to stare at her deputy. "You mean that thing is yours?"

Elvis's cheeks flushed red. "Well, not exactly."

Aloha blew out a breath and managed to get to her feet.

"I can explain, Sheriff." Annie Oakley walked over to her. "When he was a boy, Elvis planted a seedling of this particular orchid. At the time, as part of a school science program, school children were encouraged to adopt an orchid."

Aloha eyed Elvis. "I suppose it's got a name?"

His cheeks turned as red as ripe apples. He looked away toward the forty-foot high orchid swaying gently in the breeze. His eyes actually filled with tears and drooped at the corners.

"His full legal name is Fluffy Bunny Slippers." He swallowed hard, causing the bulging Adam's apple in his throat to move up and down. "I call him Fluffy."

Oh, brother. He's actually serious.

Aloha shifted her gaze to Annie. "He's kidding, right?"

She grinned, and then continued her explanation. "A lot of these orchids were raised from mutant seed provided by TZC Labs.

Unfortunately, or fortunately, depending how you look at it, the seed only germinates once."

Aloha frowned. "So TZC Labs provided the product and local school children provided the labor?"

Annie chuckled. "You catch on fast. Yes, for the next few years a hundred-and-seventy-odd giant orchids were raised and tended to by the school children, who eventually became teenagers and then adults."

"Don't tell me, when the children moved on to other interests as they grew older, the plants died off?"

Annie shook her head. "Not exactly. The abandoned plants were harvested by TZC Labs, who used the flowers in their research into a zombie cure."

Aloha considered the forewoman's words. It suddenly dawned on her. "One of the ingredients in Zombie Away is orchid flowers."

Annie nodded; obviously pleased Aloha had surmised the connection. "Initially, yes, but today a chemically manufactured synthetic is used in place of the real thing."

Aloha shook her head, and her brow wrinkled. "Then I still don't get it."

"The roots." Hanson interrupted them, his voice muffled by the grass from where he lay face down with his hands handcuffed behind his back.

"Get him on his feet," Aloha instructed Elvis, who immediately grabbed Hanson's right forearm and pulled him to his feet. Elvis held him. Hanson spat out blades of grass that had lodged in his mouth.

"What about the roots, Mr. Braddock?" Aloha moved closer to Hanson, and it surprised her when her heart rate increased. While her annoyance meter was on the rise, her sudden close proximity to the handsome restaurateur had set off her pheromone alarm.

Talk about your mixed emotions. She hadn't been this confused since she broke it off with Matt, and he was half zombie.

"They're destroying the wall." His lips formed a thin line, and his eyes flicked to Elvis, then back to her.

Aloha looked at Matt. "This true?"

Elvis winced. "Sorta?"

Aloha threw her arms up in the air. "What? The wall is the only thing stopping the zombies from escaping! Take the handcuffs off Hanson. Now."

Elvis's features flushed bright crimson; he did as he was told. After the handcuffs were off, he took a step back and to the right of Hanson.

Hanson Braddock alternately rubbed each wrist and smiled at Aloha. Only his smile wasn't born from humor. It was one of those smiles the director of L.I.P.S. too often gave her that twisted her stomach into knots and caused her sleepless nights. He wasn't very happy with her.

"So, Mr. Braddock, what do we *have* to do?" she said.

Without responding, Hanson walked to where the double-headed axe had fallen when Aloha tackled him. He picked it up, swung it over his right shoulder, and ran a hand through his shoulder-length hair. He winked. "Me and Max are gonna cut down that orchid."

"Who's Max?"

Hanson turned and walked away with a chuckle. "It's what I call my axe, Sheriff."

Do the guys in this town name everything? Aloha glanced at the forewoman, who wore a puppy dog smile on her lips.

"Isn't he wonderful?" Annie sighed.

Oh, brother. Get her. Aloha looked back at Hanson, who now stood at the base of the giant mutant flower.

43

He set the axe head on the grass, leaning the handle against his right leg, spat in his hands, rubbed them together, then gripped the axe handle in both hands and hefted the heavy tool into the air. The flower wouldn't know what hit it.

"Yup, he's pretty wonderful," Aloha, said sarcastically.

Out of the corner of one eye she caught Annie's brief glare at her and smiled to herself.

Take that, lady. He's not yours.

With one swing, the orchid came down.

Behind Aloha Elvis started to cry.

~~~

Aloha studied the hole in the dome wall. It was certainly large enough for a person to slip through, but they'd have to work at it.

Annie and her team impressed Aloha with their skill and work ethic. She could see the sweat trickling down their faces through the visors of their protective suits as they worked to prepare a special patching compound to close the hole.

Annie explained the rip in the wall had been patched three times in the past week but that each time within a day or two the hole reappeared. And it seemed as if the compound had never been applied.

The compound was a mixture of silicone, wall plaster, super glue, and peppermint-flavored toothpaste. Developed by TZC Labs forty years ago, it had never failed before. Why it failed now was definitely a mystery.

Two of the crew climbed up the scaffolding to the platform nearest the top edge of the tear six feet above the ground. Even then they would have to reach over their heads in order to apply the compound.

Annie stood at the base of scaffold with the other crewmember.

Her faceplate was tilted back as she watched her people struggling to fill the tear with two oversized trowels that required both hands to maneuver.

Aloha and Elvis stood far enough away that the fumes from the compound wouldn't envelope them. Annie had warned them the fumes could render a person unconscious if inhaled, which was one reason the work crew wore the protective suits. The forewoman didn't explain but Aloha assumed another reason had something to do with whatever was on the other side of the dome wall.

She didn't believe the story about there being another dimension on the other side of the wall, but she couldn't be sure either. She hadn't believed in zombies either until she met one.

The two crewmembers working overhead had filled half the tear when they stopped and let the tips of their trowels drop to the platform. Aloha could see their arms trembling, and their shoulders were slumped in exhaustion.

They carefully set the trowels on the platform and climbed down. After they reached the ground, Annie and the other crewmember scrabbled up the scaffolding and began to work.

One of the workers walked over to join Elvis and Aloha. When he took off the helmet of his suit, she saw the worker was male. He was breathing hard, and his flushed features were bathed in sweat, the scent of which grew more pronounced as he drew closer.

He offered a weary smile as he stopped beside her and ran his fingers through his soaked hair. He held his helmet under his left arm. Aloha acknowledged the man with a nod and a tight-lipped smile. Her self-consciousness about her too-tight uniform made her cross her arms to hide the swell of her bosom. She shifted her gaze back at Annie and the other worker busily, almost frantically, working compound into the other half of the tear.

"We've been at this for three days," he said.

"Yes. Annie told me."

"Never happened before."

Aloha nodded.

"Now, that's different." He said it so casually that at first Aloha didn't register what she was seeing, but then her eyes narrowed, and her heart began to pound in her chest as adrenaline flowed into her blood stream.

One thing she never tired of was the action part of her job description. Only problem was she didn't know what action to take right now.

As they watched the patch, Annie disappeared into the tear in the fourth wall. The oversized trowel the forewoman had been holding clattered onto the wooden planks when its owner was sucked soundlessly into the void beyond.

Chapter Six

ELVIS STEERED THE LARGE PICKUP truck into the gravel parking lot off Piano Lane, which ran along the back of the two-story City Hall complex. He pulled into the reserved stall for the sheriff, right in front of the back entrance. The horseshoe-shaped campus reminded Aloha of the L.I.P.S. Academy. Gravel crunched under the tires as the truck came to a stop.

It annoyed her when Elvis wanted to stop for coffee before coming back to the office. Forty-minute coffee breaks were so going to be history. Annie had disappeared. Finding her had to be the priority — not a coffee break. Aloha hoped finding Annie would lead her to what happened to her predecessor and to Elvis's brother. Somehow she suspected finding one missing person would create a domino effect.

Eying the deputy she wondered why he didn't seem worried about Annie's sudden disappearance. *Strange.*

The rumble of the truck's V8 engine faded to an echo off the two-story brick building's walls after Elvis cut the engine. A stuffed roadrunner toy hung off the end of his brass key ring in the shape of a large E.

He swiveled in his seat and glared at Aloha. "You shouldn't have let Hanson chop down my Fluffy."

"Why? Are the plants important?"

Elvis shot her a look of indignation. "Everything's connected, Sheriff. The dome, Fluffy, Annie, Sheriff Bradley, my brother." His eyes narrowed, and she saw his knuckles turn white as his grip tightened on the misshapen steering wheel. "If the dome is destroyed, not only will the zombies get loose but the fourth dimension will intrude into our world, and I don't know for sure what will happen, but I don't think it will end well."

Aloha suspected he was right, but Hanson had been adamant the roots of the giant mutant plant had created the tear in the wall. At least Hanson was half way rational, Elvis wasn't rational at all when it came to his plant. Now that she'd seen with her own eyes what happened to Annie, she thought the plants had nothing to do with the impending doom of Zomopolis. The cause wasn't natural. Something was very rotten in Denmark and Zomopolis.

Her gut sense was an evil force was at the heart of this mess, and the knot in the pit of her stomach told her time was not on her side.

If Arnold Zero and his power-crazed clan weren't still serving time on the Prison Wars reality television show, she might suspect their involvement. Imagine releasing dangerous criminals for the sake of ratings on a TV show. What had the world come to? If only she ran the world things would be *very* different. But she had a job to do and it didn't involve running the world.

Of course, if this had nothing to do with Zero, then there was a new kid on the block, and that was bad news for everyone, especially the Woman from L.I.P.S.

"Sorry, Big E. I hope you can forgive me."

Evidenced by the deep scowl on his wide features and the grim line of his mouth, Aloha knew his answer before he spoke.

"I'm gonna have to think about it."

Aloha wanted to sigh but held back, unsure how he would react if she showed her relief. She'd only been on the job a week, and she needed him since he'd been the deputy for so long. She hoped he wouldn't leave her to save the world alone. One L.I.P.S. agent could only do so much, even with Dr. Oh's top-secret gadgets. She was beginning to think she would need all hands on deck if she hoped to complete the mission successfully.

Though, come to think of it, Aloha had no idea how long Elvis had been the deputy. But she did know it was longer than she'd been sheriff.

"How long have you been the deputy of Zomopolis?"

Elvis didn't speak for several seconds. She thought he wasn't going to respond, when his features relaxed and the tension bled off in his shoulders as they drooped slightly. He looked away toward the building, turned left, and started to walk toward the tree-filled public park to the left of the brick building. Through the window of the truck, Aloha heard birds calling to each other from the tall fir and cypress trees that populated the park.

"I've been the deputy for ten years." The big man dropped his hands from the misshapen steering wheel.

Aloha sighed and nodded. "Do you sometimes miss the previous sheriff?"

"Yeah."

The L.I.P.S. briefing report said her predecessor had disappeared under mysterious circumstances over a year ago. The report didn't have much on Elvis, other than he was a local boy, so she was going to keep tabs on him. A few questions she already knew the answers to might loosen him up, at least she hoped.

L.I.P.S. Director Simon Mynass had assigned her to this case because she had experience finding lost things and people who lost them. And of course she had gotten to know a few zombies during her last case, so she had the experience Director Mynass had been looking for.

After breaking up with her zombie ex-boyfriend she'd had her fill of the undead, but orders were orders, so L.I.P.S. Agent Aloha Armstrong became sheriff of Zomopolis for as long as it took to find Sheriff Bradley. And to discover who or what was behind her predecessor's sudden disappearance.

The only thing really tingling her spy senses her was if that mad megalomaniac Arnold Zero really was somewhere involved in the strange events in this town. *That midget creep has been a thorn in my big toe for years, so if there's trouble in Zomopolis I expect I'll find him nearby.*

"Tell me what happened to him." She looked toward the park to add the illusion she wasn't interrogating him, which in fact she was. And it might give her a clue as to what happened to Annie Oakley too.

Elvis eased back against the seat cushion. "Sheriff Bradley was a great man."

"I'm sure he was, but why are you talking about him in the past tense?"

Elvis sighed heavily. "The day he disappeared he called me on the radio saying he was headed out to check on an urgent call from the dome repair crew in sector five."

"Sector five?"

Elvis nodded. "Yeah. It follows four, ya know."

Aloha smirked.

"Anyway, the sheriff never called me again. Ever." His eyes filled with tears.

"Did you try to find him?"

Elvis snorted and swiped across his eyes with the back of his right hand. "Of course I did." His voice was thick with emotion and edged with bitterness. "We mobilized every able-bodied man and woman in town and searched for three days. Nothing. Not a trace. Nothing," he added again.

"What did Billy Buick say?"

Elvis shook his head. "He said he called Sheriff Bradley requesting he come out to sector five right away."

"And you don't believe him?"

Elvis shook his head again.

If someone else called, then Billy was covering for someone, but whom?

Strange. The previous sheriff disappears under mysterious circumstance two months ago, and then the fourth wall begins to break down. Now Annie Oakley disappears. The link between them was the fourth wall and the cracks. Aloha had been unable to save Annie, but she had to find out what was going on and stop it before the entire town, and maybe the rest of the world, disappeared into the fourth dimension. A lot was at stake, more than she originally thought the mission objective called for.

Her head was swimming with all this mystery. She grunted and then swung the truck door open and got out. The gravel crunched underfoot as she walked to the entrance. Once on the cement pad in front of the door she tapped one boot at a time against the cement lip surrounding the pad to shake off excess dirt from the soles of her boots. She'd changed back into her cop boots after they'd returned to Elvis's truck.

Elvis came up behind her and pulled the door open and held it for her waving one hand for her to enter first, She paused to eye her deputy before she walked past him. What was Elvis's involvement in all this? He'd been the deputy when the disappearances started, yet here he still was. Could she really trust him to be telling her the full truth and nothing but the truth? For the first time she wondered if the net gun really had malfunctioned or he had wanted the zombie to take her out.

The metallic tinge of gravel mingled with the tangy odor of fir trees wafting over them was replaced with the smell of dusty carpets, copier ink, and floor polish.

They made their way down the carpeted hallway past open office doors where the mailroom and the counter service staff sat when not serving townsfolk who came in to pay their property taxes or buy their dog licenses.

Aloha stuck her head into the office and said hello to Ethel Schmidt. Ethel looked over the reading glasses perched on the end of her bulbous nose. Ethel had been the one who showed Aloha around on her first day. She was a portly, matronly woman with a head of tightly permed and dyed blonde hair. Ethel had a Minnesotan accent and was a real charmer and incredibly intelligent. Aloha was certain people underestimated her because of her accent. Something Ethel no doubt used to good advantage.

"Ya! Hello, Sheriff. Good ta see ya." The corners of her eyes wrinkled as she smiled. "How's she goin'?"

"Fine, Ethel. Just fine."

Ethel's smile disappeared. Her generous mouth formed a grim line. "Not what's I bin hearin'."

Aloha nodded and left Ethel's office without saying another word. Hard to argue when someone was right.

"I'm going to see the mayor," she told Elvis after they were alone in the elevator and the door had closed. "You get started on the missing persons report."

Elvis shrugged. "Annie's not missin'."

Aloha's brow wrinkled. What was that supposed to mean? "She's not in this dimension, Elvis, is she?" The deputy nodded. "Just write the report anyway, OK?"

"You're the boss."

The elevator door slid open, and Elvis's cowboy boots made the familiar heavy thump on the thin carpet as he walked away, and she turned toward the mayor's office. His grunt of reproach followed him.

He didn't agree with her. *And I'm OK with that.*

Yes, Big E, she was the sheriff. Discovering who was behind these events was her job, and of course finding Sheriff Bradley was too. *And a L.I.P.S. agent never fails. Never.* She always got her man, woman, or whatever.

~~~

The mayor of Zomopolis, Sharona Figer, former high school basketball star and underwear model, was town gossip extraordinaire.

On the second day on the job, Aloha made the mistake of telling Sharona she was a natural redhead, and she learned how quickly news got around town.

Half an hour later she sat in Joe's having lunch, and three people including the waitress mentioned her natural red hair. When Hanson came up came up to her and whispered in her ear he loved natural redheads she knew immediately who had told him.

Aloha released the breath she'd been holding and swung the mayor's office door inward.

53

Behind the reception desk sat Max "Crash" Hawker. His blue-and-red-striped bow tie sat at the base of his long, lean neck. His perfectly pressed suit was buttoned in the middle as usual, and he sat in his orange ergonomic office chair with his back rigid. If you looked up the definition of ninety-degree angle Aloha was certain you'd see Crash's picture.

He regarded her dully over the top edge of his black-framed glasses that sat near the tip of his long nose. His cold gray eyes narrowed slightly with recognition.

"Do you have an appointment?" His reedy voice had taken some getting used to, but Crash exuded efficiency from his pores.

"Huh, no, Crash, but this is an emergency." He winced at her use of his nickname. Deep inside her the stuffed shirt's discomfort pleased her.

"That's what they *all* say," Crash responded drily recovering from her *nom de* too familiar.

"But this time, Crash, Annie Oakley's missing." Annie may not have been truly missing but the reality, or rather the unreality of inter-dimensional travel would have taken too long to explain.

Crash stared at her but didn't respond. She realized he didn't know who Annie Oakley was so decided she'd better elaborate. "The patching compound for the dome wall is failing."

His thin lips pursed. He still wasn't convinced.

"The zombies are going to escape."

The thin brown eyebrows on Crash's pale forehead rose in unison. "Why didn't you say so?"

He rose from his chair and walked to the door to the inner office. As he walked he unbuttoned his suit jacket and swept one side open to reveal a white and navy-blue proximity card hanging off a red plastic accordion key ring attached to his belt.

He pulled the card up and swiped it once across the proximity card reader next to the door. Aloha heard a soft click as the door lock disengaged.

Crash let go of the proximity card, and it snapped back to his belt. He swung the door open with the flat of his right hand while he re-buttoned his jacket with the fingers of the other.

Amazing. Not one wasted move. "Madam Mayor. May I have a moment?"

Aloha heard the mayor say OK from the ceiling above her. Crash swiveled his head to look at her. "Wait here, please."

Aloha shrugged and nodded. *Like I have a choice.*

Crash left reception, entering the mayor's office and closing the door behind him. Aloha found she was alone in the reception area. She took a seat on one of the two faux wood-framed chairs sitting on either side of a large green cactus.

There were no magazines so she fidgeted in the chair and crossed and uncrossed her legs several times until after what seemed like an eternity the door to the inner office opened and Crash came out. His expression told her nothing.

After closing the mayor's office door he took his seat behind his desk and cleared his throat. She stood in anticipation of going into the mayor's office and began to form the right words in her mind to tell Sharona the highlights of what would be in her report of the day's events.

"The mayor says she has a spot next Tuesday from 11:03 until 11:13 to meet with you, Sheriff. Hopefully you have nothing pressing on your calendar at that time; otherwise the next available slot is in three months."

"You did tell her it's an emergency? Life and death, right?"

His eyes narrowed. "I don't recall any reference to life and death."

She thought for a second and realized he was right. She hadn't said those exact words, but the escaping of the undead through the fourth dimension certainly qualified as an apocalyptic event for someone. Rumors at L.I.P.S. HQ were the fourth dimension led into her world. She wasn't convinced this was true since she'd never seen any evidence to support it, but it was her duty to protect the citizens of every dimension not just the one she lived in. An impending apocalypse was about as life and death as it got, and, after all, fourth-dimensionites were people too (or so she hoped).

She lowered her voice. "Crash, I don't have time for word games, and I can't wait until Tuesday. I have to see the mayor *now*."

Crash glared at her, and his cheeks flushed, but he remained seated with his hands flat on the desk. "Tuesday," he said between gritted teeth.

Aloha looked to the proximity card reader next to the door. It seemed the mayor was obsessed with security. *You'd think she was the freakin' president,* thought Aloha.

She released the safety strap over her pistol's trigger guard, and then withdrew the weapon from the holster. She didn't have time for this crap. And no pipsqueak assistant was going to stand in her way when it was a matter of life and death.

"Crash, I'm not going to wait and certainly not until Tuesday. My business with the mayor is of the life-and-death variety. I'm the sheriff, and it's my job to warn the town, and the mayor is in charge of the town, so if you don't let me in right now I'm going in anyway."

To emphasize her point she unsnapped the button on a compartment on her gun belt and pulled out a three-inch steel projectile with a rounded base and a pointed tip. Dr. Oh said this projectile, specifically engineered to fit in the barrel of her Glock, was designed to destroy any lock without damaging the door or the surrounding walls. He guaranteed nothing nor anyone would be injured even if they were standing listening on the other side of the door.

Crash rose from his chair and waved his hands. "No, Sheriff! Don't do something you'll regret."

Aloha offered the mayor's assistant a crooked smile as she slipped the projectile into the firing chamber of the gun. It made a *snap* sound as it locked in place. She'd never tried it before. She hoped it worked as advertised.

Shifting her eyes to the prox reader, she raised the weapon and took aim. "Move back, Crash."

Crash stood up behind his desk; his bird-like features were purple as a concord grape. "Sheriff! Do not shoot that lock!"

Aloha's eyes narrowed, and she took a shooting stance with both hands gripping the heavy plastic butt of the Glock. The boom of the gun going off drowned out Crash's yell as he rushed around the desk intending to stop her. The projectile shot out of the barrel, sheathed in flame, and covered the distance in a millisecond.

With a deep thud and a loud bang the proximity card reader shattered into bits of flying plastic and shredded wires that scattered across the carpet. Crash dropped to his stomach with his arms and hands protecting his head. The debris fell around and over him like snow.

In the quiet that followed, there was a soft click as the door lock disengaged. *What do you know it actually worked.*

Aloha stared at the shattered prox card reader. But in hindsight, Dr. Oh's invention did seem a little like overkill. She shrugged. *Oh, well, in for a penny in for overkill.*

Aloha rushed past a red-faced Crash, who lay prone on the floor, lowered one shoulder and hit the door at full speed. With a loud bang and the tearing of screws, the metal hinges shrieking, the door tore loose and slammed hard into the wall. The door seemed a little flimsy. *Maybe the prox card lock was a decoy?*

Aloha stumbled into Sharona's office, her gun held at the ready position. The smell of exploded rocket fuel filled her nostrils. The acidic taste filled her mouth when her jaw fell open. Sharona wasn't alone. She heard the mayor's voice from somewhere in front of her in the smoke. "What's going on here? Who's there?"

Waving the smoke away Aloha's breath caught in her throat when the smoke cleared enough to reveal the sight of a coughing, bare-chested Hanson Braddock standing facing a painter's easel, his lean body with its six-pack abs in a bodybuilder pose. Behind the easel a red-faced very angry Sharona, with a paintbrush gripped between her teeth, a color palette in her hand and a black beret tilted at an angle perched on her nest of dirty blonde curls, glared at her. *Hanson and Sharona? What the...?*

"What's going on in here?" Aloha said between gritted teeth. She had assumed Hanson and she had connected on a deeper level. *Guess I was wrong.*

Chapter Seven

HANSON STARED AT ALOHA where she stood framed by the smoking ruins of the shattered door frame.

Sharona coughed.

"Hey!" The mayor covered her mouth with her fist and bent forward coughing harder.

Hanson's surprise finally registered, and he blinked then dropped his arms to his sides. "Aloha! What's going on? Have the zombies gotten out of control again?" Hanson walked to the chair where he'd laid his navy t-shirt across the back and snatched it up.

If the zoms were on the warpath his cafe was in danger. He had to get over there right away before they wrecked the place. He pulled the t-shirt over his head and started toward the door. He waved away smoke from his face with one hand.

"Hold on there, mister," Aloha said between gritted teeth. She stepped into the room and into a wide stance. The gun with the barrel still trailing smoke hung at her side. She held out one hand to stop him in his tracks. "Where do you think you're going?"

Hanson stopped and glared at the sheriff. She was acting as if he were the one who destroyed the door. "Get out of my way, Sheriff. I've got to get to the restaurant right away before they wreck the place."

Aloha didn't move, but she lowered her hand. "What are you talking about? Who are *they*?"

Hanson considered her question and realized she hadn't actually said the zoms were rioting, had she? His tension dissipated, and his cheeks grew warm. "There is no zombie attack. Is there?"

Hanson watched Aloha shake her head and holster her pistol.

"Sheriff!" Sharona's cheeks and her pink one-piece jumpsuit were smudged with smoke, and her eyes burned with anger. Aloha's usually cocky manner disappeared, and her normally robust features paled.

"Yes, Mayor?"

He liked this new side to the sheriff. He had thought she was hot since the moment he had laid eyes on her, but vulnerability was definitely the new sexy.

Sharona adjusted the beret on her head and then marched to stand in front of the sheriff with her hands on her hips. Since the mayor was six inches shorter than Aloha she had to tilt her head back to glare up at her.

"Aloha," she breathed, "I hired you because your experience as a former federal agent involved with paranormal investigations makes you uniquely qualified to handle the zombie situation here in Zomopolis."

Aloha's eyes flitted to Hanson then back to Sharona.

Sharona's left foot began to tap out a beat. She crossed her arms. "What I didn't expect was you'd break into my office and very nearly kill me!" The mayor shouted the last part.

Crash suddenly burst into the room. His clothes were soiled by smoke; his tie hung loose form his open-necked shirt. And his normally perfect hair looked like it had been combed with an eggbeater.

"Mayor! Mayor!" he gasped. He was breathing hard, and his eyes were wild with fear.

Now what? thought Hanson.

The mayor's forehead wrinkled and she scowled at her assistant. "Crash, what's wrong?"

"Attack..." he blurted, then stumbled to the mayor's desk and used it to keep himself from falling.

Aloha took a step toward him, her features deadly serious, her eyes on fire. "Who?" she said. "Where?"

Her right hand enveloped the butt of her pistol and thumbed off the leather strap over the trigger guard. Aloha would pull the gun out if she needed it. She visibly tensed, and her eyes narrowed and became watchful.

Wow, she's good. He loved a woman of action. Hanson eyed her up and down in her form-fitting uniform. And what a woman! *Whew!*

"Downstairs... Elvis... called..." His brow was beaded with perspiration. With a *whump* the air burst out of his lungs, and he moved to sit in an empty chair in front of the mayor's desk. He loosened his tie, and his breathing began to slow.

Aloha yanked her cell phone out of the leather case on the belt surrounding her narrow waist. She flipped it open and raised it to her ear.

"Talk to me, Elvis," she said simply.

When Aloha snapped her cell phone closed and grunted, the look in her eye was of someone far away, her mind working on a problem.

Silence. Sharona looked directly at Hanson, her expression unreadable. Hanson grew increasingly uncomfortable in the silence. *What the heck is going on?*

Finally she spoke. "Well, Aloha. What's happening?"

This broke Aloha's concentration. "Huh?" She nodded. "Yes, of course. It seems we have a slight problem."

"I know that. Crash already said." Sharona scowled and placed her free hand on her hip.

Hanson smiled to himself. *Ever feisty.* He had to love that about her.

Aloha frowned. "A gang called the Wanderers has invaded the building. Elvis tells me they're zoms, and I'm wondering how I'm going to stop them without using my gun."

~~~

Aloha avoided the elevators; instead she led Hanson to the stairs. He'd volunteered to help her. She reluctantly accepted his assistance after he assured her he had once been in the military and could handle himself in a fight. He'd twice saved her life already, so she figured she owed him some consideration. Besides he explained she would need the help with this gang of zombies; they had had a bloodthirsty reputation before they were locked up in Zomopolis.

If the skateboarding undead teens were waiting outside the elevator doors when they opened she'd be forced to do something she wanted to avoid. Namely, she'd be forced to shoot one of the zoms in the head to stop their rampage.

But her orders from the mayor were quite clear: shoot a zombie and you're fired. Yeah, that was about as clear as it got. Normally she'd ignore orders from a politician, but she had a job to do. If she were fired, her mission would be a failure. And L.I.P.S. agents never failed.

She stopped on the grate-like steel step and strained to listen for any signs of the zoms coming from below or above.

"What're we doing?" whispered Hanson.

He stood one step behind and above her. His aftershave wafted over her.

Even his scent was a heady mixture of salty sweat and cinnamon spice. She frowned and scolded herself for losing concentration on the mission at hand. She couldn't afford any personal entanglements right now. Their lives were at stake.

The sound of two boys laughing made her tense. Her right hand moved instinctively to the pistol in the holster on her hip. The sound of steel wheels on cement followed, then the slam of a door. Aloha's heart raced, and beads of perspiration dotted her forehead.

"What's happening?" whispered Hanson, his tone urgent.

"The Wanderers are at the bottom of stairs."

"So? They're gone now, aren't they?"

Aloha turned her eyes to lock with his. "Yeah. But they know we're coming."

His eyes grew wide. "How?"

A crease formed on Aloha's brow. "I'm not sure, but I have my suspicions." Elvis was her prime suspect. He grew up in this town, and he knew the zoms better than anyone. She suspected he even had friends among the zombies.

The Wanderers were a group of teenage zombies who skateboarded around town. They were victims of the army chemical weapon tests in the 1950s and had stayed as undead teenagers since they were turned.

In the '50s the Wanderers' membership numbered in the hundreds.

A top-secret government project isolated the zoms in detention centers that were the foundation of towns like Zomopolis. After the invention of Zombie Away all of these towns, except Zomopolis, were closed.

Now Zomopolis' reason for existence was dedicated to finding a cure for the remaining zoms.

In 1991 The Totally Zip Corporation was awarded the U.S. government contract to set up a research facility in town. TZC hired scientists from around the world to work on a zombie cure for the remaining zombies. So far they'd been unsuccessful.

The three Wanderers now rampaging on the first floor were all that remained of the hundreds of teenage zoms. The rest had been cured.

The good thing they were chemical zombies so she wasn't in danger of being eaten since they were vegetarians. At least her brain was safe. *Good thing I don't carry broccoli in my pockets though if you made them made even a veggie-zom can be dangerous.* The Wanderers had proven that over the years. A large enough herd of chem zoms was capable of stripping a supermarket of fresh produce in record time. If the magical zoms and the chem zoms teamed up to form one massive herd then all life — both animal and vegetable — on Earth would disappear forever. All that would remain would be mineral — and you can't eat rocks.

She released a breath and realized she'd been holding it for the last several seconds. Her firearms instructor always told her to breathe normally when you're about to fire. If indeed she had to fire on anyone, if it came to that. She really didn't like gun play.

Signaling with two fingers of her right hand she started down the stairs. After taking two steps she stopped to listen. Other than her heart beating in her ears the only sound was Hanson's breathing. He was nervous.

"You OK?" she whispered.

"Yeah. Fine." The tone in his voice told her he was lying.

Don't sweat it, big guy. When you don't grow up with zombies being the norm, even one can be scary.

They reached the bottom step. The gray walls and floor were made of cement. The floor was beveled, and in the center was a drain covered by a round steel grate about three inches in diameter.

To their right and left were steel fire doors painted neutral beige. *Hmm... Door number-one or door number-two?*

A loud *bang* made her start and crouch lower. Her fingers gripped the pistol butt tighter, and her heart beat faster.

She hated threats she couldn't see.

Hanson joined her, his runners making a soft squeak when he stepped off the bottom step onto the cement floor. "That noise came from behind door number two."

Aloha looked at him and grinned. *Can he read minds?* She chuckled uneasily. "Which one is door number two?"

Chapter Eight

WHEN NOTHING HAPPENED AFTER SEVERAL minutes and there were no more strange banging sounds Aloha decided they would go out the door where there had been no sound, it offering a better chance of escape.

There was no point in walking into an ambush.

The two fire doors were identical. Both were made of steel; both were painted an identical shade of beige. The biggest difference was one led to the hallway on the first floor, the other to the outside.

If she and Hanson went through the door into the hallway the zoms would have the high ground and the advantage. She needed to assess the damage and see where they were. If she could get to her office she'd be able to use the zombie proximity detector to locate the Wanderers loose within the building. Once she knew where they were, then she'd be able to plan a strategy to contain them.

When zombies went bad, they went really bad.

The door had a stainless steel panic bar. She pressed it down, and the door swung outward. She stuck her head out and blinked in the bright sunlight. Her vision adjusted, and she looked both ways down the side of the building. The door emptied onto a green space with young maple and birch trees; a duck pond and wooden picnic tables were scattered around the park-like space.

She stepped onto the grass; it compressed under her boots.

It was hard to believe they were under attack. The park was so peaceful. Several small birds flitted by overhead, chattering as they flew.

"Wow. This is nice," said Hanson, who had stepped out the door behind her. She looked over her shoulder in time to see him let go of the heavy steel door.

Aloha winced when the door banged shut. "Did you have to do that?"

"Do what?" said Hanson, his tone laced with indignation.

"Hey! They're over here!" shouted a young boy from the left side of the building.

Aloha couldn't see them but she knew they were coming. The Wanderers. "The door. You let it close."

She glared at Hanson. The sound of the metal door closing would've echoed up the staircase to every floor in the building.

Even so it still seemed unlikely the zoms would be outside waiting for them. Aloha reached to the pouch on her gun belt where she kept Dr. Oh's secret weapons. She pulled out a packet of gum. She pulled out the last stick from the package. Unwrapping it revealed the gum was bright neon green.

Hanson looked at her, his forehead furrowed.

She grinned. "Gum?"

He shook his head, and one corner of his mouth curled into an uneasy smile, but this was no ordinary stick of green gum. *Little do you or these zoms know, pal.*

"Hey, Flattop! I found 'em!" yelled a young male voice.

Aloha looked to her left just as two young zombies appeared from around the side of the building. They each carried a fiberglass skateboard tucked under their arms.

One skateboard was a bright orange and the other an electric blue. Their baseball caps were turned around on their heads, and they wore black t-shirts, one with a red dragon design, the other with a white eagle with its wings spread.

Their sunken eyes were the color of coal, and their faces were ash gray.

"Hey, dudes," said one of the young zoms who sauntered arrogantly toward them. *They must think we're easy prey.*

The zom who spoke's sneering lips were a darker gray than his face. "How's it hangin'?"

Well, think again, buddy.

The other zombie grunted and started toward them but was veering gradually off to their left.

"Do I look like a dude?" said Aloha, emphasizing her sex by tossing her long red curls about her shoulders.

They're boxing us in like they're a pride of lions and we're the gazelles. I'm a lot of things but I'm not that easy.

Hanson's eye's flitted to her, then back at the slowly approaching zombies. He whispered, "I thought you said they were from the fifties. I hate to state the obvious but these two look more Tony Hawk than James Dean."

Aloha looked at him and smiled. "I only get the advertising, not the details." She chuckled. "I'm new in town. Remember?"

Hanson's cheeks reddened. He was cute when he was embarrassed. She liked him, but she would have liked him more if he'd had some weapons training.

"Yeah. Sorry. I forgot." He turned away from her toward the zombie circling them. Likewise Aloha turned her attention to the one approaching head on. "What're we gonna do?"

"You're gonna die, dudes," growled the zombie with the dragon on his skateboard. He pulled off his ball cap and tossed it to his left. It landed on the well-groomed lawn near the base of a recently planted birch sapling.

Die? She didn't think so. The zom's handle was certainly clear. Its dark hair was cut in the best flattop she'd ever seen. Impressive. *You could land a plane on that doo.* She wondered who cut the zom's hair. *It could be a clue.* She shelved the thought for later. Right now she had a few undead assesses to kick.

The zom moved closer, and as he did he raised his skateboard in front of him at chest level.

What the heck was he doing? The zom's mouth formed a sly smile, and his eyes narrowed. Aloha heard a click, and a blade appeared from one end of the skateboard. The thin blade, sharp on both sides like a razor, with a tip that looked capable of piercing flesh with one thrust, frightened her as much as the zom's intense eyes. Sunlight glinted off the finely honed steel as he slowly approached them like a hungry lion stalking a potential kill.

Oh, oh... he's gonna slice us up like sushi. Aloha's body tensed, and her heart began to beat hard in her chest.

"Do you see that?" said Hanson, his voice edged with raw fear.

"Yeah," she said, "I see it."

Looking at the gum in her hand she hoped Dr. Oh's weapon worked. She squeezed the stick of gum, crumpling it into a ball in her fist.

She looked up at the zom, and her mouth formed a half smile as one side of her mouth curled. The zom suddenly broke into a run as he raised the skateboard knife above his head. He emitted a shrill war cry as he came at them faster and faster.

Aloha stole a glance at the second zom and saw he had stopped moving and was watching the action intently.

Good. He thought his partner was going to make short work of them on his own. "Follow my lead," she instructed Hanson.

Aloha unfurled her fist and rifled the rolled-up gum at the charging, screaming zombie teen. It struck him in the center of his t-shirt in the open mouth of the dragon design.

The zom came to an abrupt stop and stared at the ball of gum in the center of his thin chest. When nothing happened after a few seconds he looked up at Aloha and laughed.

"What's up, babe?" His eyes narrowed. "If the gum messes up my shirt you're sooo gonna pay."

Aloha crossed her arms and grinned. "I don't think so, zombie-boy."

"What the...?" The zom stared down at the gum. The gum had begun to expand rapidly from a small ball of green to cover his chest and upper torso and quickly covered him from his neck down to his legs until it finally covered his head. His scream disappeared as his mouth and nose were covered in a layer of green. He fell backward and lay still in a cocoon of gum.

Aloha glanced at the second zom and smiled to herself. *That ought do it.* Dr. Oh rocked. "You want some gum?"

The second zom stood still, frozen in place, his eyes flitting between Aloha and the large green cocoon encasing his now helpless friend. His eyes were wide with surprise, and his mouth hung open. His lean frame and his hands were trembling. Suddenly he stopped shaking and stared at her.

What's he up to? The remaining zom lowered the skateboard under his arm and his index finger pressed something underneath the board where the wheels were affixed.

Aloha's heart rate climbed. She didn't like the look in his eye.

It was then a thick blade popped out from the end of the board with a dull *thunk*. "These guys have the Swiss army knives of skateboards, eh?" she murmured softly.

"No kidding," agreed Hanson, about whom she'd nearly forgotten. "He looks a little pissed."

Now she detected his aftershave. "Cool Breeze," she said. It had a slightly mint finish. She knew this because her former boyfriend wore Cool Breeze aftershave. The scent reminded her of snuggling with him in front of a roaring fire at the ski lodge the day he told her he was marrying another woman for her money. He at least had been gracious enough to offer her a position as his mistress.

After planting a well-placed kick in his behind, Aloha, being Aloha, had declined the gracious offer.

"How did you know?"

"Remind me to tell you sometime." Aloha nodded toward the zom walking toward them with the business end of the skateboard glinting in the sun. Just as with the other zom's blade, this one too looked sharp, very sharp.

Aloha's muscles tightened. The adrenaline was really flowing now. Her heart pounded in her chest, but her hands were steady and her breathing under control. It was like the good old days at L.I.P.S. academy when Ilsa had ambushed her in the showers. She smiled to herself. She really kicked her butt. It felt so good.

"By the way *it* is not a he. *It* is an undead monster who happens to look like a *he*."

"What?"

"You said he looks pissed. Zombies do not get pissed or happy or sad. They're dead people come back to life by chemical or magical means.

The half-made ones eat the same food we do, but they don't enjoy it. The flesh-eating ones eat humans, mostly brains. The chem zom's are vegetarians, but you can't let them near a supermarket."

Hanson's eyes narrowed. "How do you know this stuff? I thought you just got to town?"

"I did." She couldn't very well tell him about her L.I.P.S. mission briefing could she. She was undercover, after all.

"Got more gum?" asked Hanson, changing the subject when she didn't elaborate. The skateboard-wielding zombie was only twenty feet away now and was preparing to strike.

She shook her head. "Sorry, fresh out." Truth was she had more back at her house but she'd forgotten to reload. Her eyes narrowed. "Guess we have to take on this zom the old-fashioned way.

"Which is?"

Funny. He doesn't seem as scared as before. She was pretty sure if she weren't a L.I.P.S. agent she'd be scared.

"Suicide run."

Aloha took two steps closer to the zombie and stuck her thumbs in her ears. "Nah, nah, nah, you're it!" She stuck her tongue out and blew a raspberry.

The zombie snarled and suddenly burst into a run while screaming at the top of its lungs. It ran right at her, waving the knife end of the skateboard wildly.

She had him just where she wanted him. *Oh yeah, baby.*

"Hey! Sheriff! Watch out!" Hanson came up beside her, breathing hard, his eyes wild.

Oh, oh. She had a bad feeling about this turn of events. She opened her mouth to speak, but before she could say anything Hanson ran headlong at the zombie.

Oh, crap! What was he doing? "Hanson, stop!" she yelled. She ran after him.

Before she could stop him, Hanson and the zombie met, and Hanson threw a left cross that struck the zombie across his chin. The zombie stumbled backward a couple of steps and shook its head as if to clear the cobwebs, but it didn't lower the board.

Boy, Hanson sure packed a punch. *He better watch that skateboard knife though.* Just as she finished the thought, the zombie shoved the blade into Hanson's midsection. From this angle, she couldn't tell exactly where he'd been struck.

"No!" she shouted. The zom didn't look up as she came up to it. She used her pistol butt to drop the zombie with one sharp blow to the side of its head. It crumpled into a heap at their feet. It was out cold. The knife board fell out of its hands, and the blade buried itself in grass.

Aloha grabbed Hanson's shoulder and spun him around to face her. His blood-covered hands were over a wound in his stomach. Blood leaked between his fingers. His face was white, and his eyes showed the pain and shock. He was trembling.

Oh, man that doesn't look good. If she didn't do something he was going to die. She couldn't help herself. She had begun to have feelings for the guy. Her heart pounded against her ribs. He couldn't die, not now. Her throat tightened. *What's the matter with me?* She'd saved the world and millions of lives as a L.I.P.S agent, yet one man's life had her choked up.

Struggling to stay the fear from her voice she said, "Don't worry, Hanson. I'm gonna get help."

Finally her mind shifted to the problems at hand and her L.I.P.S. training kicked in. Problem number one: Where was she going to get help?

The zombie lying on the grass rolled onto its side and moaned softly. Problem number two: What if he woke up before she returned with help?

"Everybody freeze," said a deep voice from behind her. Aloha's heart skipped a beat, and she stood still, keeping her arms loose at her sides.

Now what?

Chapter Nine

A S HE'D EXPECTED HE was stabbed before he dropped the zombie. His fingers and toes were cold and growing colder with each passing second. He was losing blood from the wound in his stomach. He needed help soon or.... He didn't want to think about dying. At least not yet.

Aloha was on her knees beside him. She had taken off her jacket and laid it underneath his head as a pillow.

"You'll be OK," she whispered.

He didn't believe her, but he wasn't about to give up either.

"I'm going to get help," she said and then stood.

Hanson grabbed her by one ankle. "No," he said between gritted teeth. Sweat poured off his forehead into his eyes, stinging them. He blinked to clear his vision.

"I won't be long," she said. "Trust me."

The sincerity in her voice made him feel better. He let go of her ankle.

"I'm going to tie these zombies up before I go." She squatted beside him and removed his belt from his pants. "I'll need this."

He blinked and managed to see the small tight smile on her lips and the twinkle in her eyes.

He sighed and nodded. A feeling of euphoria came over him. He could sleep for a week. Suddenly there was a burst of pain so intense it felt like his guts were caught in a lawnmower. He passed out.

~~~

Awaking in the dark Hanson wondered where he was. Shifting his legs he realized he lay on a bed. But why was the room dark?

"He's awake."

A woman's voice? But whose? "Hello?" he said. What the...? His voice sounded like he'd swallowed sandpaper.

"I'll be right back, Mr. Braddock. The sheriff's explained everything."

"Yeah, OK."

He snorted. Why couldn't he see anything? Had he lost his sight? *I was stabbed in the chest not in the eyes.* This didn't make sense.

He heard a door swing open and the familiar snap of leather cowboy boots on tiles. And he smelled her perfume, Cinnamon Bun Revival. He'd know that smell anywhere, sweet and sexy. Aloha Armstrong had entered the room.

"Hey, Aloha. How's it hangin'?"

"I'll be OK, Nurse." He heard Aloha say. "You run along and do whatever else you have to do. I'll take it from here."

"How…?" the nurse started to say and then paused. "Yes, Sheriff. Of course." The door opened again, and there was a barely audible squeak of rubber-soled shoes, and then the door thumped closed.

"Hope you didn't upset her," he said. "You could be the one in here next, ya know."

Aloha chuckled, and he heard her move closer to his side. The scent of her perfume was stronger.

"Yeah, but at least I'm not the one suffering from hysterical blindness."

"What's that? I'm not hysterical; I'm freakin' blind."

"Well, you may not be hysterical right now, big guy. But you sure were the other day."

The other day? "How long have I been in here?"

"Three days."

A surge of panic shot through him. *I'm getting hysterical now.* "Three days? Will my eyesight return?"

"Don't worry, Hanson, the doc assures me you'll be seeing just fine very soon. In fact he thinks your sight will return today." After a short pause she added, "At least I hope so."

Hanson's sense of panic was eased slightly by her reassuring words. *She really cares about me.* A change of topic was in order.

The scrape of a chair being pulled across the tiled floor made him start, and then he heard the sigh of the cushion, meaning she had sat down. Aloha obviously was planning to stay awhile. Not that he objected. Now she had saved his life, just as he had saved hers. She'd repaid him in full.

"We're even, ya know," he said.

"I know," she said simply.

She was no conversationalist that much was clear. "By the way, Hanson, I meant to thank you." At the edge of his vision he saw a gray formless shape appear. His vision had started to improve. Aloha had eased his mind. Her being so close was obviously good for him. *Interesting.*

Hanson started when he felt her close to him, then the soft brush of her lips on his cheek and the warmth of her breath against his skin.

"Thank you," she whispered. A feeling of disappointment came over him as she moved away.

"You OK?" she said.

He chuckled uneasily. "Uhhh, yeah, I guess so."

He winced when a sharp pain in his abdomen reminded him of his recent stabbing. He took in a deep breath then let out the air to slip between his lips as the pain receded. "I guess it only hurts when I chuckle."

"Isn't that only when you laugh?"

"Cliché," he explained, offering a wry grin but refraining from chuckling, or laughing. The fogginess that clouded his vision had begun to clear. A sense of relief washed over him. The blindness had indeed been temporary. He could see her distinctly feminine curves now and was glad she hadn't had time to alter her uniform.

"Well, Hanson, you get better soon. You've got a lot of hungry customers that need feeding. I've got to go."

"Yes, I understand. You have a case to solve, am I right?"

"Uhhh, yes. How do you know?"

He shrugged. He could make out her face now. It was still in shadow, but he could see her expression of curiosity. Her eyes narrowed. "You're a secret agent. Sharona said you work for something called the Legal Investigative Protection Service. You must be the Jane Bond of spies."

He could see her clearly now, and his heart skipped a beat. She looked even more beautiful than when he'd last seen her. Was it the good drugs or had his vision suddenly improved?

Aloha's features relaxed. She laughed, deepening the dimples on her cheeks. Her eyes seemed to twinkle, sending a shiver through him. "I used to be a federal agent. They used to call me the Woman from L.I.P.S. But that was used to be.

Now I'm a small-town sheriff with —" she paused. "*Unique* skills," she finished. "I don't do that spy stuff anymore."

"Wanna talk about it?" he said, hoping she would. Being a real life spy had to be cool. It sure looked cool in the movies.

The corners of her mouth sagged, and she shook her head and looked away. He'd hit an abrasion point. "Sorry," he said. " I didn't mean —"

"No, no," she interrupted him, "don't be silly. It's not you. It's me."

Oh, oh, he thought. *I've heard that from one too many former girlfriends.*

"Anyway," she said before he could speak. "I have to go. I'm late already."

"See you later?" he said, hopefully.

The dimpled smile reached her eyes in record time. "Sure. I'll see you later. I'll drop by before I go home. OK?"

He nodded and licked his lips, hoping he wasn't being too obvious he really liked her. *But now is not the time*, he cautioned himself. Danger first. Dating second.

Then she turned away and was gone. The door thumped as it closed behind her. He was alone.

He realized he had grown feelings for her, and he hoped she cared about him beyond the fact he'd been wounded on her watch. He frowned. Until then, he hadn't considered the possibility she felt responsible for his injury and wasn't interested in him beyond that.

Chapter Ten

ALOHA WALKED INTO THE HOSPITAL parking lot and stopped as she came to the replacement vehicle the town had provided for her. It was ridiculous and totally unacceptable to make her drive such a silly car. The Huvo looked like the kind of car clowns popped out of at the circus.

She sighed and got in. She turned the key to the on position and waited. It still unnerved her that the Huvo made no sound at all. A car that ran silent was just plain wrong.

Imagine Steve McQueen or Bruce Willis tearing up the streets driving cars that made no engine sounds, no roaring engines, and no grinding of gears and looked a ridiculous as this car did. Movie chases would become the boring part of any action movie. All that would be left would be the ridiculous gunfights where the guns never ran out of bullets. Or shooters turning their guns sideways before they fired.

Yeah, right, then the searing hot shell casings hit you in the eye and blinded you? Stupid. That stuff in the movies still drove her nuts. Being a real action hero made it hard to enjoy action movies, but she still loved them regardless.

She put the car in reverse and backed out of the parking spot and then shifted to drive and started going to the entrance to Violin Lane. She had to be at TZC for a meeting Sharona had arranged with the director, Dr. Seymour Schlock.

As she drove she wondered if Hanson liked movies? Maybe he'd like to go with her to a movie sometime. She grinned. *I hope he enjoys dumb action movies as much as I do.*

She arrived at the Totally Zip Corporation main gate within twenty minutes of leaving the hospital. The guard was a broad-shouldered black man with a gold tooth. His eyes were wide when she stopped the Huvo in front of the drop-down gate. He stepped out of his booth with a clipboard in one hand.

She hit the button to roll down the driver's side window. It rolled down half way and stopped. No matter how many times she pressed the button, it stayed where it was and wouldn't go up again so she and the window were both stuck.

"Hello," she said cheerily.

"Uhhh, hello. Sheriff?" The plastic name tag on his uniform read *F. Barston.*

She nodded. "Yes. I have an appointment with Dr. Schlock." She struggled to keep her tone light and cheerful. The stupid car had really made her mad.

Barston looked bewildered but glanced at the clipboard. "Yes, of course. I'll raise the gate so you can dri—I mean go inside."

Aloha felt her face grow warm. She really had to talk to Sharona about the ridiculous toy car. How would anyone respect her position of sheriff with such a car?

"Thanks, Barston."

He stepped inside and flicked a switch. The gate came up quickly with a *swish.*

She smiled and nodded and stepped on the go pedal. The little car leapt forward, and she passed him. He nodded and smiled, then went back to the newspaper he'd been reading when she drove up to the entrance.

Aloha shook her head and grimaced.

She found a single empty parking spot in front of the building with "administration" in large red letters over the lobby doors. At least something was going right today. If she hadn't found this spot she would have had to park and walk back, and who knew how far away that would have been. Over half the town worked at TZC, so parking was at a premium.

Surprisingly, she was worried about Hanson. He was a very nice guy and had saved her life. In some ways she owed him. After her bad experience with Matt she had sworn off men, but there was something about Hanson she liked.

Maybe it was his sense of humor or his good looks or his strong commitment to right over wrong. He had certainly made a difference at the diner when he'd lassoed that rampaging zombie.

After stepping out of the Huvo, she closed the door and hit the button on the controller attached to her key ring. There was a single beep, which meant the locks had engaged. Not that she was worried anyone would steal the thing.

Any man who defeated a zom was a man with skills, and she liked skills. It seemed odd he hadn't showed any skills at City Hall during the Wanderers attack.

She walked to a main entrance comprised of twin oak doors that reminded her of the doors to an ancient castle. Affixed to one of the doors was a large brass knocker in the shape of a gargoyle. She smiled to herself. *Someone has a morbid sense of humor.*

She used the knocker to announce her arrival. Recessed into the other door was a square section of wood that looked like a miniature trap door. She could even see the small brass hinges.

It startled her when the small door suddenly swung inward and a face appeared. Her breath caught in her throat.

The face was that of a zombie. A zombie she knew.

Chapter Eleven

A LOHA WANTED TO PULL HER GUN and blow the smiling face of Arnold Zero off his zombie body. But she refrained. *I knew it. I knew he was here somewhere. Will I ever shake this creep?*

Zero was a little person and madman who had tried to killed her on a previous mission. Under normal circumstances she never held a grudge against any of the criminals she arrested, but this guy had gotten under her skin. Seeing him again made her skin crawl.

But Zero had done his time and had ended up zombie-infected. The irony being the Zombie Away he'd coveted, and nearly killed her and many others to get control of, had had no effect on him. He was not only incorrigible, he was incurable.

"This way," said the little man. "I'll take you to Herr Director. He's been waiting to see you." Zero glanced back over his shoulder at her and leered. A shiver ran down her spine. Guy gave her the creeps. She'd need a shower after being anywhere near this perv.

"He's been eager to meet you since you took over as sheriff." He turned his attention to the twin glass doors they were approaching. Stenciled across the doors were the words *Administration* and *Brewery.*

Brewery? TZC has its own beer-making facility? Who knew?

"How did he know?" Aloha asked.

Zero opened the door and then stood aside to let Aloha enter ahead of him. Aloha considered hesitating, fearing that if she did Zero would be behind her and thus have the advantage, but she threw caution to the wind and went in.

I'm the sheriff, for goodness sake. Zero would never do anything to me here.

Aloha started when the glass door thudded as it closed behind her. "I'm sorry for all the trouble I created." The air smelled of hops and yeast. Pungent but not unpleasant.

Aloha stopped and turned around to face Zero, looking down as she came to a stop. She peered into his dark beady eyes. "You nearly killed me and my friends, and you are a megalomaniac. Besides, I don't like you. I think the parole board made a mistake letting you loose on the world again."

Zero smiled. "Ya got me, Sheriff." He held out his arms. "Slap the irons on and throw away the key."

Aloha couldn't help herself; she laughed. "Zero. Zero. Zero. You are a piece of work. Do you know that?"

Arnold Zero chuckled and dropped his arms to his sides. "Listen. Sheriff. I paid for my crimes, and no one got hurt." He sighed. "When I became infected and discovered the Zombie Away spray didn't work for me I thought my life was over. I thought I would end up shot in the head or burned to death or some other grisly fate, but the Zombie Away did make me half zombie, half human like it does to ninety percent of the infected."

He paused. His eyes got a faraway look in them. "That fact provided a glimmer of hope. Then I discovered the Totally Zip Corporation's research facility here in Zomopolis trying to improve Zombie Away, and now I think I have a real shot at a cure."

The corners of Aloha's mouth curled slightly and her eyes narrowed. "So you can continue your life as a super villain as if you never left?"

Zero grinned, obviously enjoying this verbal play. "You don't trust me, do you?"

"No," she said simply. She looked around the office lobby. "Where's the director's office?" Aloha had had enough of this conversation-to-nowhere with her former archenemy.

In front of her was a half wall covered with portraits of six smiling men and women, an equal number of each. Underneath each portrait were a name, and the title *director* and *chief executive officer*. Beyond the wall were rows and rows of workstations surrounded by half walls that went back as far as she *could* see. From what she *could* see of the closer workstations they were occupied by an assortment of men and women peering at computer screens or typing on computer keyboards.

"Not back there," said Zero.

Aloha regarded the little man with distain. "Zero, all I want is to meet the director. That's it."

Zero smiled. "Ok, OK, take it easy. I'll take you to his office right away." Zero walked toward a stained pine wall to the right of the reception desk. After an audible click, a section of wall swung open, beyond which was the interior of an elevator.

"Now that's different," said Aloha dryly.

Zero stood to one side and swept his arm theatrically, "After you."

Aloha smiled thinly, then walked into the elevator. The walls were made of mirrors framed with polished brass. Zero stepped in after her and pressed one of the two buttons on the panel next to the door.

The button had the letter B etched on it. The doors slid shut silently.

"What does B stand for?"

Zero smirked. "Big Boss."

"Then shouldn't it be BB?"

Glancing at the reflected image of Zero, Aloha saw him shrug. "Matter of opinion."

She looked back at her reflection in the mirror and smiled. *Score one for me.*

The elevator came to a stop, and the doors slid aside. Beyond the open doors was a luxurious office. The floor had a thick emerald-green and gray carpet. Filtered sunlight streamed in through a floor-to-ceiling window in front of which was a massive glass-topped desk.

To his right on the desk was a flat computer screen; to his left was a telephone resting in its charger.

The man stood up from his black leather executive chair and smiled widely, revealing snow-white teeth. "Sheriff. How nice of y'all ta visit me in my humble little ol' office. Name's Harlan Pepper." He came around the desk to meet her halfway from the elevator. He stuck out a suntanned hand in greeting.

Aloha took his offered hand in hers and shook it. His flesh was warm and his grip strong. His gray pinstriped suit was tailored to accentuate his lean, fit form. His accent was southern, but she couldn't place from which state exactly. "Director," she said as he released her hand. "Nice to meet you as well."

As she stepped backward, she heard a yelp. Turning around, she saw Zero, his features flushed. He was gasping in obvious pain, holding one booted foot in both hands while hopping on the other.

"You stepped on me," he croaked.

He fell backward, landing with a thump on his bottom. "Ouch!"

Aloha covered her mouth in time to stifle a laugh. "Oh, my. I'm so sorry."

Zero was one nasty piece of work. Their previous encounters had been unpleasant, to say the least, and he'd nearly killed her more than once. She had a hard time believing he was a *reformed* megalomaniac.

The director grimaced. He leaned toward her to whisper in her ear. "Good help is so hard to find these days."

She looked into his hazel eyes. Was he trying to make her laugh?

"Director Pepper, I'd like to meet you alone. We need to discuss some security issues that have arisen over the past few days."

Pepper peered at her. "Oh? Is it serious?"

Aloha's eyes narrowed. "Yes. Very."

"Well then, Sheriff, I guess we need some face time. Alone." He looked at Zero, who'd regained his feet, his breathing rapid.

Zero grunted and scowled at Aloha, then focused on the director. "Yes, Herr Director." He hobbled to the elevator, and after entering the elevator car, disappeared behind the closing doors.

Aloha disguised a giggle behind a snort.

"You shouldn't make fun of others that way," admonished Director Pepper before returning to his chair behind the massive desk.

"Do you know who he is?" Aloha asked indignantly, surprised Pepper would be defending the evil midget.

"He is my executive assistant, and part zombie."

Aloha shook her head in wonderment. Four feet in front of her a chair appeared from a hidden hatch in the floor. When she sat down she was pleasantly surprised by the soft, forgiving comfort of the chair's cushion.

"I'm sorry, Director Pepper, but that man is an evil megalomaniac whose only goal in life is to take over the world."

"I'm sorry, Sheriff, but I must disagree with you. Arnold Zero is a changed man. He's been reformed by misfortune."

Aloha saw it was useless trying to convince Pepper of Zero's true nature. Then again, maybe the little man had changed. Only time would tell. For now she'd keep an eye on him.

Maybe they clone people around here too? I'd need a few of me to straighten out this mess. Her to-do list was growing every minute of every day.

How am I going to keep an eye on Zero, while stopping a growing zombie rampage — and find a way to rescue the workers sucked into the fourth dimension?

Then there was still her missing predecessor.

Her deputy, Elvis, clearly wasn't much help. He had his own issues.

"Dim the room, Betty," said Pepper. The floor-to-ceiling windows behind him darkened, reducing the amount of light coming through. The pot lights along the ceiling became brighter.

Director Pepper removed his dark sunglasses. Aloha started and stared at the director. Pepper's eyes had pomegranate-red pupils.

Pepper smiled thinly. "An industrial accident in my youth."

"Oh. Sorry."

He waved off her apology. "Nonsense. It's not like y'all tripped me."

"No. It's not —" *Stop,* she scolded herself, *before you dig a deeper hole. You really don't want to know what happened to make him a red-eye.*

Aloha crossed her legs, and her large pistol holster banged hard against her thigh. Darned thing was oversized and heavy.

Pepper sighed and turned away from her to face the tinted windows.

"Light is an issue for me. Hence, I devoted my years to working on my mind."

"Sorry?" Aloha rubbed her thigh and blew air between her lips. "What's 'an issue'?"

"Light, sheriff." He waved one hand casually at the window. "Sunlight, specifically."

"Sunlight." She nodded. "Yeah. I burn easily, too." She pointed at her hair. "My people gotta be careful."

Pepper turned around to face her. "Sheriff. What are we talking about?"

Aloha gazed at Pepper. Her nose wrinkled. "Uhhh, sunburns?"

Pepper stared at her for several seconds until he finally said, "None of that matters, Sheriff." He sat down again in his executive chair and frowned. "I'm sure you have bigger problems."

"Yes, sir, I do. Some of the repair workers have been sucked through the fourth wall, after tears began appearing in the dome wall, and there have been increasing zombie attacks. I've been attacked myself, twice." She could have added she really liked Hanson but she wanted to keep that private, at least for now. She'd been down the road of telling-friends-about-her-feelings-about-a-man-she-liked-then-they-told-the-man-who-laughed-and-rejected-her-before-the-relationship-began. Long ago, Aloha decided she would never make that mistake again, and besides, she'd just met Harlan Pepper, they weren't friends yet.

Pepper's brow creased. "Are you OK?"

Aloha's face grew warm. "Uhhh, sorry, yeah, I'm fine. I mean… I'll be fine. My oversized holster banged against my leg, and it's nothing…" Realizing she was rambling she stopped talking.

She smiled weakly. "I'm rambling. Sorry. Seeing Zero really caught me off guard."

Pepper smiled. "Understandable. What can I do for you? Or should I say, what can TZC do for you?"

Aloha was pleased they'd finally gotten back on subject. "I understand TZC is working on a new improved version of Zombie Away."

Pepper's eyes widened. "Really? Who told you that?"

"Is it a secret?" Aloha shrugged. "I read it somewhere." Her brow wrinkled in thought. "*The New York Times* or maybe *Better Homes and Zombie?*" She looked into Pepper's red eyes and felt a little queasy. "I'm not who you think I am."

Pepper eased back in his chair, resting his arms on the arms of his chair. "Who are you then, Sheriff?"

"I'm a woman on a mission, and I'm cooperating with the feds. They've taken an interest in the goings-on in Zomopolis since my predecessor went missing." She couldn't very well reveal she was a L.I.P.S. agent.

"Really?" said Pepper. Aloha nodded as her mouth formed a thin line. "Well then, what is so interesting in Zomopolis to a federal agency that you need to be *cooperating* with them?"

Aloha hadn't thought that far ahead. "Uhhh, I'm sorry, Director, for now, that information must remain classified." She'd said as much as she dared to gain his help without revealing her true mission — time to put on the brakes before he asked too many questions. She was treading a fine line as it was.

Pepper nodded, but his expression was skeptical. "Yes, of course."

"I would appreciate a tour of your facility. It may help me in my investigation. I'm hoping your research will change the zombies before they're all out of control."

"Oh? Are they out of control?"

Aloha shook her head. "Not all of them, just a few. There was one at Hanson's diner this morning, and we encountered rampaging Wanderers at City Hall." Her eyes narrowed. "Hanson was stabbed."

"Oh, my. Is he OK?"

"Yes. But whoever is behind these attacks is going to pay." Her voice dripped with menace; startling her with the depth of feeling she had developed for Hanson.

"Was anyone else hurt?" asked Director Pepper.

Aloha took in a deep breath, then released it slowly to steady herself. Only then did she respond. "Uhhh, no…well, I was hurt a little, but I'm fine now."

"I see." Pepper moved around his desk, donning his dark sunglasses as he did. "Shall I show you around?"

"Certainly." After a short pause she added, "Thank you, Herr Director."

Pepper stopped and stared at her. "Why did you call me *Herr Director*?"

Oh, crap. What have I done now?

Chapter Twelve

THE ELEVATOR DOORS SLID OPEN silently when they reached the lowest level of the TZC complex. Surprisingly there were seventeen levels below the lobby. They were now seventeen floors underground.

Aloha had a touch of claustrophobia, so she had to steady herself and concentrate to settle her vague feeling of unease. Still, tiny beads of sweat had formed on her upper lip, and her skin felt damp underneath her uniform. It made her skin feel clammy. She hated it. She would have preferred to have a shower right now, but the tour of this facility could be important. She had her suspicions that the zombies somehow involved the TZC facility in the disappearances and the odd behavior. Involvement by Arnold Zero had ticked her mental checklist of bad stuff. Zero was at heart a maniac bent on world domination. His claim he was reformed reeked like expired milk.

Pepper glanced at her. The presence of those dark sunglasses increased her discomfort. The eyes are the windows to what a person is thinking, and the dark glasses hid a lot of emotion. Not that his red pupils were all that pleasant to look at.

"Claustrophobic?"

She wondered if he could read minds. She'd seen stranger things in her time as a L.I.P.S. agent. She nodded.

"Yes," he said with a nod, "it does affect some people this far underground." He stepped out of the elevator without looking back. "Please follow me."

Aloha swallowed, then exited the elevator and started to follow. She looked up at the ceiling that rose some twenty feet overhead and immediately felt better. Her cheeks puffed out as she blew air from her lungs.

The vast underground spread out before her was filled with large whitewashed vats. The floors were highly polished cement coated with a substance that sealed them so dust and dirt wouldn't adhere to the surface.

Workers, some with clipboards, dressed in white jumpsuits, their shoes covered with plastic shields, moved among the tanks, stopping on occasion to study a gauge then write something on paper on their clipboards.

The scene made her think of a James Bond super villain's lair. She had begun to suspect Director Pepper might be just such a super villain. Red eyes, armed security guards, a window that changes color — in her experience these were all the signs of the megalomaniac-want-to-take-over-the-world types she'd met before.

Her suspicions were confirmed when she noticed some workers, without clipboards, carried sidearm's in holsters at their waists.

Pepper led her across the vast and surprisingly quiet room, past the tanks, to a door marked *Research and Development.*

"In here, please," said Pepper, before opening the door and entering first. Aloha entered after him, pulling the door closed behind her. It was a laboratory, all right.

Long lab tables, with seemingly randomly placed Bunsen burners, supported test tubes and different sizes and shapes of beakers containing a multitude of colored liquids from ruby-red to emerald-green. Men and women, and even a few zombies wearing glowing headbands, were bent over the tables peering at bubbling liquids in beakers and pouring test tubes half filled with other liquids or powders into each other. *He has found a way to control Zombies. Impressive.*

One man wearing dark goggles stood at the end of one table behind what looked like a laser cannon from a *Star Wars* movie. He peered at a block of steel held in place by a vice.

"Is he going to fire that thing?" Aloha wondered out loud.

"Oh, yes, indeed he is…" Pepper hesitated and his brow wrinkled. "Am I supposed to call you 'Sheriff' or something else?"

Aloha chuckled to cover her embarrassment. "Aloha. Just call me Aloha."

Director Pepper looked at her for a few seconds and then nodded. "Yes, *Aloha*, the technician is going to fire the laser at that block of pseudo-steel." He turned away to gaze at the technician, who was making the final adjustments to the laser.

Pseudo-steel? What's that?

The technician glanced at Pepper, who nodded. The technician adjusted his goggles, and then his index finger hovered over a red button sticking up from the back of the laser. Aloha noticed his finger was trembling. Beads of perspiration dotted his forehead.

The technician pushed the button, and the laser began to hum, softly at first, then gradually louder and louder until Aloha was forced to cover her ears. Her features were squished like she'd sucked on a lemon. Her eyes were now slits, but she could see the sound didn't appear to have affected Director Pepper.

Suddenly a beam of blue light shot out of the laser, hitting the piece of pseudo-steel dead center. At first nothing happened. Then the steel began to change color — first a fiery red, then yellow, and finally a brilliant sapphire blue until it suddenly exploded.

Aloha dropped to lie on her stomach, covering her head with her arms. "Incoming!" she warned.

"Aloha," said a man's calm voice. "You can get up off the floor."

Aloha slowly uncovered her head and looked up to see Director Pepper standing over her. He had his arms crossed and one eyebrow cocked; one side of his mouth was slightly curled upward.

Aloha got up, brushing imaginary dust off her uniform. The place was like a hospital it was so clean. Her face felt warm. "But what about the explosion?" She looked where the block of pseudo-steel had been and saw all that remained were piles of shrapnel in the shape of an invisible box. Aloha frowned. "Force field?"

"Yes, Sheriff, we use them quite a bit around here. Tends to keep the place tidy."

"But how did the laser get through the force field?"

The director offered her a tight smile. "That's a trade secret, I'm afraid."

"Oh." A trade secret? Secret from her? Her business was keeping secrets. *Like my undercover identity.* She winced. *Oh, brother.*

"The pseudo-steel is a new material created to increase the strength of the dome wall. Unfortunately, the laser caused it to explode in this test so we have to go back to the drawing board. Our goal is to make the dome indestructible." He looked at the technician, who nodded and left them alone.

Now this was something she appreciated. They were working on replacing the dome, and since the dome was developing cracks, this was a great thing. "That sounds good to me, given what I saw."

Pepper's brow wrinkled. For a fleeting second Aloha thought she'd like to read the expression in his eyes, then discarded the idea. Those red eyes were creepy.

"What did you see, Sheriff?"

"I saw Annie Oakley, forewoman of the repair team, disappear through a tear in the dome wall. My deputy says his brother also disappeared in similar circumstances."

"But you didn't see his brother disappear?" asked Pepper.

Aloha shook her head.

"Interesting." Pepper turned away. "Let me show you the research laboratory where we're working on the new improved Zombie Away."

There's another lab after this one? "Is it on another floor?" she asked.

"No, not exactly."

Why did Pepper have to be so cryptic? Yeah, he was doing some good stuff, like trying to strengthen the dome wall, but then he had to speak in *cryptoese*. This added to her conviction Pepper was a super villain. Problem was: how did you prove someone was a super villain before they did something villainous?

Aloha followed Pepper to a rear wall that was bare of any adornments. He pressed his hand flat against a spot on the wall. There was a barely audible click, and then a section of the wall swung inward.

First Pepper has red eyes, then he speaks cryptically, and then he has hidden doors. All super villain-type clichés. The evidence was building.

Aloha decided she better be on her extra-special guard around this man.

"After you," he offered, standing aside to let her go ahead of him.

Aloha paused and peered into the room on the other side of the doorway. The laboratory beyond appeared to be identical to the one they were in now except there were no lab technicians, at least that she could see.

Suddenly her cell phone chimed its familiar moose calls.

She glanced at Pepper and saw him tense. *Oh, man, I thought I left my cell on vibrate.* She pulled her cell phone from her pocket. The tiny screen showed it was Elvis calling her. She thumbed the green button and brought the phone to her ear. "Hi, Big E, what's up?"

She listened intently for several seconds, and then pressed the red *off* button that ended the call. "Sorry, Director, but I have to go. Duty calls."

"Problem?"

"Nothing serious, but my deputy needs my help." She walked away, headed for the elevator. She had to restrain the urge to break into a sprint.

Director Pepper closed the door to the second laboratory and hurried after her.

They entered the elevator and rode up to the lobby. After shaking Pepper's hand, Aloha said she'd be back and then walked to the parking lot. She got in, started her car, and sped as fast as the tiny car could manage. The emergency lights affixed to the roll bar on the roof of the car flashed, reflecting off the houses and shops as she pasted. Cars and trucks pulled off to the side of the road to let her pass.

The car's electric engine began to hum louder and louder in her ears, and her nostrils and mouth filled with the slight odor of acrid smoke. The tiny engine was being strained to its limits. Glancing at the speedometer she saw the car had barely achieved forty miles an hour. This confirmed she better not get in any car chases with anything faster than a scooter.

What she hadn't revealed to Director Pepper is Elvis was serious, very serious about abiding by speed limits. According to the briefing file on him he'd issued more speeding tickets in one year in this small town than an LA freeway cop. A gang of thieves was holed up in the bank. Elvis radioed he'd come across an SUV with tinted windows car, it's engine running, parked in a no-parking zone in front of the First Zomopolis City Bank.

Elvis called her saying had pulled up behind the SUV, intending to write a ticket. When he approached the driver's side, he could see the truck's window was rolled down, revealing what looked like a zombie behind the wheel pointing a double-barreled sawed-off shotgun at him.

Elvis barely dove to the street in time to escape being shot before the driver fired. The SUV then roared off with a screech of tires and disappeared around the corner of Bassoon Road and Obo Street.

As he got up and began to dust himself off, two hooded men exited the bank and fired handguns at him. Elvis managed to get behind cover and exchanged several shots with them until the two men retreated into the bank.

That's where he was now — outside the bank waiting for her. His tone had been surprisingly calm.

Zombies robbing banks, Aloha mused while steering the tiny car around a corner, *what will happen next in this crazy town?*

Chapter Thirteen

ALOHA ARRIVED JUST AS THE BANK robbers opened fire again. Elvis, seated on the pavement his eyes hidden behind his sunglasses beside his pickup truck with his back against the rear passenger-side tire didn't move or look in her direction. He seemed to be ignoring her.

To avoid being shot exiting her car, she steered the tiny car toward an alley across from the bank. She'd leave her car there and run to join her deputy using whatever cover she could find to guard her approach. As she neared the alley way a figure stepped from the shadows not ten feet in front of the car. She held her breath, and her heart rate increased. She was going to run someone down.

Not if I can help it.

Yelling to the stranger to get out of the way, she closed her eyes and used both feet to press down hard on the brake pedal. The little car fishtailed but came to a stop accompanied by the echo of screeching brakes off the alley's high brick walls

Breathing hard, she opened her eyes to see the smiling features of Hanson Braddock peering back at her. He rapped his knuckles on the driver's side window.

Aloha frowned and pressed the button on the door that opened the window. "What are you doing here?" she asked after the window was open.

"Well, hello to you too."

"Sorry, but don't you hear the shooting? It's dangerous around here."

He nodded, and there was a twinkle in his eyes that she could feel as much as she could see. "I know. I was minding my own business walking along this street," he locked eyes with her, "after I broke out of the hospital, when I came across Elvis being shot at from someone in an SUV," He shrugged. "I thought I would help."

Aloha nodded. Hanson's observations matched what Elvis had told her. She'd doubted the reliability of her deputy. This meant he'd told her the truth. It was a good sign. "Then what happened?" she asked, as she turned off the car's engine. Her shoulders relaxed.

He shook his head. "Not important. Why don't we go see what's happened? The shooting has stopped."

Aloha realized he was right. The shooting had stopped. Her heart beat harder. *Elvis?* Now she was worried. He could be dead.

She threw open the car door, forcing Hanson to take a step back, then stepped out and led the way to the mouth of the alley. She kept her back against the wall and edged to the corner. She smiled to herself when she heard Hanson's footsteps following her.

He was definitely growing on her. *Walking by the bank, my butt. He must have a police scanner and picked up Elvis's radio call.* Hanson Braddock had secrets. She intended to find out what they were.

Once at the corner she stole a peek around the wall. Her heart froze when she saw Elvis slumped against his truck. His eyes were closed. He wasn't moving, but she didn't see any blood.

What she also didn't see were the bank robbers, but the SUV Elvis described was still parked outside the bank, and the smoke from the tailpipe meant it was still running. Where had the bad guys gone? Were they still in the bank or the truck?

Strange for zombies to rob a bank. Why would the undead need cash? It wasn't like they had credit cards. In her L.I.P.S. briefing package she read the government provided everything they needed while they lived in Zomopolis.

Oh, oh. Her cheeks grew cool. Maybe they were planning a dome breakout? If that were true then she was going to need a lot more help.

This was not going well. Her hands were shaking. She took in a deep breath to steady her nerves.

Aloha leaned back against the alley wall. The brick was cool on her bare arms and her hands. A breeze from the alley entrance carried with it the faint tinge of burnt gunpowder reminding her of the recent gun battle.

"What is it?" whispered Hanson. "Is Elvis OK?"

Aloha glanced at him. "I don't know."

"What are we gonna do?"

Aloha considered her options. What should she do? Maybe that small package she received a few days ago from Dr. Oh Elvis put in the trunk of the car had something she could use to save her deputy? In all the excitement she hadn't had time to check everything the doc sent her. The doc's briefings were so long winded her mind too often wandered. She figured press the button, pull the trigger, or whatever, cross your fingers, and hope for the best. It worked for other spies so why not her?

"Let's go back to the car. No one dies on my watch, especially my deputy."

Hanson's features drooped, and he stared at her, his eyes wide. "What about Elvis? And the bank robbers, what about them?"

"No worries. I have a few tricks up my sleeve." *At least I hope Dr. Oh does.* Hanson shrugged and followed her down the alley to the car.

Aloha pulled out her car keys and pressed the unlock button for the trunk on her key ring. There was an audible click and the trunk opened revealing the small satchel-type bag Dr. Oh had couriered her. The satchel reminded her of an old-fashioned doctor's bag she'd seen in old movies.

After opening it she found it contained only two things. What looked like a flashlight and an odd-looking gun with a black metal tank that ran across the length of the barrel. She picked up the gun first and found it surprisingly light in her hand. The tank must have been constructed of a very light metal. She ran a finger over it to determine what it was made of. The unknown metal felt more like carbon steel than aluminum. *Interesting.*

Studying the gun more closely, she didn't see a clip in the frame or anywhere to load ammunition, and the barrel was devoid of any manufacturer markings. How did she load it?

"It looks like a kid's water gun," said Hanson. His tone suggested amusement.

Aloha had to agree; the thing did look a little like a toy. "Yeah." At least it had a trigger. She raised the gun and aimed at the wall, then pulled the trigger. A beam of bright red light shot out of the end of the barrel. The wall turned white almost immediately. Aloha released the trigger, and the beam shut off.

Hanson walked to the wall and waved his hand. He yanked back his hand as if it were on fire. "Hey! It's cold."

Aloha frowned. "I know what this is." She'd read a briefing paper on the subject of advanced non-lethal weapons research and some early tests in Dr. Oh's lab. "It's a freeze ray." She smiled. "This might be just the thing I need to save Big E."

"Wow, really? Cool," said Hanson. "What about the flashlight thing? What does it do?"

Aloha went back to the satchel to retrieve the flashlight, if that was what it was, which she doubted. She picked it up and pointed it at the wall opposite the wall that was still covered in a thin layer of ice and pressed the on button on the top of the unit. There was a soft but steady hum before the wall began to shimmer. It reminded her of her time in the desert.

In the heat the sand would shimmer and she'd think she was seeing water, or monkeys, or handsome desert sheiks riding white stallions coming to whisk her away on some romantic adventure. She sighed.

"You OK?" asked Hanson, jolting her back to the present.

She scowled at him. "Why do you keep asking me if I'm OK?"

"Sorry, lady, but you get a far away look in your eyes sometimes, and I get worried you may be suffering a concussion after the accident with the truck."

Aloha's face grew warm. "Uhhh, yeah, sorry." She looked at the spot on the wall where she'd aimed the flashlight. It was still shimmering. Stepping forward, she held one hand out in front of her. As she got closer she felt a wave of heat wash over her cheeks.

Heck of a way to get a suntan.

Dropping her arm to her side, she glanced over her shoulder at Hanson. "Heat ray." Hanson nodded, but his eyes were wide.

Aloha's heart went out to him. She'd been a L.I.P.S. agent for so long she sometimes forgot how strange weapons — and megalomaniacal evil geniuses — were all in her day-to-day work. For a civilian, such fantastic things could be overwhelming.

"You OK, Hanson?"

"Yeah. I guess so."

Her impression was he was uncertain. "Well, don't worry about all this. I'm the Woman from L.I.P.S. don't forget. I can handle just about anything." Her eyes narrowed and she straightened her shoulders. "Not even zombie bank robbers can beat Aloha Armstrong."

Aloha went back to the bag and found the tool belt specially designed to hold the gun and the flashlight. She strapped it on and placed the two weapons in the appropriate holsters.

"Let's go," she said. "But remember you stay behind me. Understand?"

Hanson nodded.

Once they reached the entrance to the street, Aloha stopped and placed her back against the wall. She then stole a look around the corner. Elvis was still, his back against the truck; his head sagged to his chest. Aloha peered at her deputy, pleased to see his chest was moving. *Good, he's still breathing.*

Taking in a breath and holding it, she crouched low, and then raced in a zigzag pattern across the open space to the side of the truck. She'd expected to be fired upon, but she made it without a shot. Still breathing hard, Hanson had managed to keep up and now stood beside her. They were hidden behind the bulk of the truck.

Aloha knelt next to Elvis to check him for wounds. His eyes were closed. Suddenly he snorted and grumbled some unintelligible words.

Oh, no he's delirious. She placed the palm of one hand on his forehead to check for a fever, but his skin was cool. Odd. Gunshot victims usually had an elevated temperature as the body fought off infections in open wounds.

But he has no visible wounds. She ran a hand across his back to check his back. Nothing, no evidence of any damage whatsoever.

Aloha sat back on her haunches and studied Elvis.

"Something wrong?" whispered Hanson.

"I don't think so." She reached out and patted his cheek with the palm of her left hand. Elvis moaned and swatted at her.

Aloha looked at Hanson, who watched her with rapt attention. She smiled to herself. *I think I have his attention. Cool.*

Suddenly she slapped Elvis with the back of her hand.

His eyes flew open, and he snorted and struggled to sit up. "Hey! What's going on?"

Aloha smiled. "What's going on is you're not dead."

Elvis blinked away the remaining sleep and yawned. "What? Who said I was dead?"

Hanson chuckled and placed a hand on Elvis's shoulder. "I guess you can sleep through anything — even a gun battle."

"Yeah, of course; my folks raised me next to a rail yard. I learned to sleep anywhere, anytime since I was knee high to my pet beagle."

The smile disappeared from Aloha's features. "But the bank robbers, they could escape while you were asleep, couldn't they?"

Elvis yawned again and stretched his arms over his head, then scratched his chest through his shirt. Aloha couldn't believe her eyes.

Her deputy regarded her sleepily. "Do you see any bullet holes in my truck?"

111

Aloha crossed her arms over her chest. She scanned the truck. To her surprise there was no evidence of damage by gunfire. What? How was it possible? She'd heard gunfire, lots of gunfire. And Hanson had as well.

"No, I don't see any bullet holes," she said dryly.

"That's because of the force screen I set up around the bank. And the SUV."

"Why the SUV?" asked Hanson.

"The rest of the gang in the truck," Elvis said, an edge of smugness in his tone.

Aloha eyed her deputy. Was Elvis also an undercover secret agent? If he was, whom was he working for? She hoped it wasn't the Big Underworld Terror and Tyranny Society or her problems had just multiplied tenfold. The B.U.T.T.S.'s sole goal was to take over the world, and L.I.P.S. fought to stop them. As a L.I.P.S. agent she had been all over the B.U.T.T.S. so many times she'd lost count.

"What force screen?" she asked.

"The one I set up when the shooting started."

This was headed down the road to *huh?* She needed to get to the facts.

She frowned. "Where did you get a force screen?"

Elvis looked at her, his face reflecting surprise at the force behind her tone.

She realized she might have come on a little too strong. "Sorry," she said, "it's just that I need to know where a small-town deputy would get such a sophisticated piece of technology."

Elvis snorted. "No worries, Sheriff, some little guy came by the station the other day with a box. He said it was a gift to the sheriff's department from TZC Director Pepper."

"And this little guy, as you call him, did he tell you his name?"

112

Elvis smiled. "Yeah. Nerdy name. Arnold Zero. Who names their kid Arnold these days? Kid must have been a bully punching bag in the school yard."

Aloha glanced at Hanson. "Yeah, who would do that? I gather the force shield device was in the box?" Elvis nodded. "And the box was small, no more than four by four. Correct?" Elvis's face registered his surprise, but he nodded again.

Aloha looked at Hanson and explained. "We have similar devices."

Elvis's eyes narrowed. "Who's 'we'?"

She'd done it again. *Do I tell Big E I'm an undercover federal agent?* She decided the time wasn't right yet; she still wasn't sure of his allegiances, and she had to be sure of his loyalty before she told him about her mission.

"Cool," said Hanson, with obvious appreciation of her organization and its capabilities. Aloha liked that in a man. "I could sure use one of them at my restaurant. You know, in case the zombies attack again."

She eyed her deputy. The weapon had come from Zero, or was it from TZC? She had trouble believing anything Zero said, no matter Director Pepper's assurances to the contrary, so she doubted the device actually came from TZC. And if this were true, then where did Zero get one? She hated so many unanswered questions.

"We better get to capturing those bank-robbing zombies and saving the hostages," Aloha said.

"What hostages?" said Elvis.

Aloha looked at her deputy. "No hostages?"

He shook his head. *Assume. I have to stop making assumptions Director Mynass would have my ass if he knew I'd made assumptions.* "Well then, what are we waiting for?'"

Elvis shrugged and stood up. Hanson offered her a lopsided grin that sent a shiver through her. Tousled dark curly hair, bedroom eyes, and a smile that could stop traffic had too often been her weakness.

"Let's go, guys. We got some zombie butt-kicking to do."

Chapter Fourteen

E LVIS HAD THE FORCE-SCREEN GENERATOR in the bed of his pickup truck. He scrambled in and pressed the red button. The unit was the size of a four-slice toaster, with an LED screen on the top bracketed by two colored buttons. The green button was *on* (or *go*, if you prefer), while red was *off* (it had to be *stop*, right?). The designer had kept the controls simple enough for the layman (or laywoman) to use. Agents didn't get a lot of classroom time for new technologies, so keep-it-simple-stupid instructions were best.

Before Elvis turned the force screen off, he said the screen told him the device was generating a megawatt of energy to create an impenetrable force that encompassed the bank like a blanket. Bullets and living matter would be dissolved if they came into contact with the force screen.

Aloha was impressed. *Good things really do come in small packages, unless their name is Arnold Zero.*

With the shield off, they could enter the bank and capture the zombies safely, or at least as safely as one could when around brain-munching zombies. From the numbers of spent shell casings it looked like an army had been in a firefight around the bank.

The force shield had dissolved the bullets, but the number of casings meant there was a good chance they'd used up all their ammunition. It explained why Elvis had been sleeping — he'd been waiting for the bank robbers to use up their bullets, and he'd known they wouldn't escape.

Aloha studied the SUV. The absence of exhaust from the tailpipe meant the truck wasn't running any longer. A good sign because the zoms wouldn't just drive off when they realized the force screen had disappeared. She signaled Hanson and Elvis to stay where they were while she reconnoitered for the presence of flesh eaters, or veggie eaters. She still wasn't sure which zombie types they were dealing with, so she hesitated to jump to any conclusions.

Unable to see inside due to the shaded windows, Aloha moved stealthily up to the rear of the vehicle. She crouched down and listened for any sounds from inside. The smell of cheese permeated the air around the truck, but that wasn't unusual. Both types of zombies loved cheese. No one knew why, but zombies were real cheese heads.

Slowly, she moved down the side of the vehicle, careful to stay below the windows with her back against the cool steel and her freeze ray out at the ready.

When she reached the driver's side door she stopped and listened again. The odor of cheese was stronger now. Her razor sharp L.I.P.S.-trained senses told her the zombies were close, as did her nostrils.

Aloha wrapped her fingers tightly around the butt of the gun, leaving her index finger along the barrel ready to move to the trigger and get off a fast shot.

You don't have to yell freeze with this baby, she thought, *one shot and you're a Popsicle.*

With the fingers of her free hand, she gripped the door handle of the SUV. She held her breath and counted to three, then pulled the handle up hard.

Ouch! It was locked. Yanking a locked door handle hurt more than she'd imagined. She holstered her gun and blew on her fingers.

"It doesn't open that way."

Hanson? Glancing toward the sound of his voice she found him smiling at her from the rear of the truck. "Well, don't just stand there, help me."

Hanson chuckled, crouched low, and made his way to the door of the truck.

When he looked at her there was a distinct twinkle in his eyes, and the laugh lines on either side of his eyes seemed deeper. Aloha shook off the thought. *I've got Hanson-itis real bad.*

Hanson knocked on the truck's door. "Yeah." Came the reply from inside the truck.

What? Could it really be as simple as knocking?

"Hey, big guy, or guys as the case may be, how're ya doin' in there?"

"Good."

"Great. Then you guys open the door and surrender. Right?"

"Why would we do that?" said the voice on the other side of the door, followed by a harsh laugh.

Hanson stole a quick look at Aloha. She offered him a weak smile. He grinned, then his eyes shifted back to the truck door. "Because there's a bomb under your truck that's about to go off."

"You're lying," said the voice. Aloha sensed uncertainty in the zom's tone.

"Really? Well, tell you what I'm going to do — I'll leave you guys with the bomb."

Aloha looked at Hanson with a wide grin on her face. "Sheriff, I think we'll need the big broom because we're going to have a lot of little zombie bits to sweep up after it goes off. And besides I'd rather not be caught in the awesome explosion. Man, there's enough bang-bang powder in this thing to equal the Hiroshima explosion. It's gonna be better than the Fourth of July in Washington."

Aloha slapped him on the arm. "Yup, sure enough, Deputy, but will the big broom do the job?" She mouthed, *bang-bang powder?*

Hanson grinned and shrugged.

Aloha covered her mouth in time to stifle a burst of laughter.

He leaned toward her. "You think I oversold it?" he whispered.

They froze as the door clicked and slowly began to swing open. Hanson held one finger over his closed mouth.

Suddenly he leaped to his feet, raised his arms above his head, and shouted, "Boom!"

Two screaming zombies fell out of the truck and onto the pavement in a heap of tangled limbs, swearing and struggling to disentangle themselves.

Aloha crossed her arms and shook her head in disgust. "Tsk-tsk. It would have been easier to sweep them up than this mess.

Hanson had impressed her. He was so cool all she wanted to do was squeeze him in a big hug.

"There you go, Sheriff, make 'em freeze."

Aloha uncrossed her arms, took out her gun again, and aimed it at the two terrified zombies, who had stopped struggling to stare at her. She pulled the trigger. The cloud of cold enveloped them, and they stopped moving. They were now covered in a thin layer of frost and ice, their eyes still open.

I love the smell of frozen zombie in the morning. Aloha holstered her gun. "Let's clean house in the bank."

"This is going to be fun," said Hanson eagerly.

She offered him a crooked smile. "You betcha, H."

~~~

Elvis joined them, and the capture went smoother than she thought it would. Any one of them would have been able to handle the task just fine.

The two remaining zombie bank robbers must have been watching what happened to their compatriots in the SUV because as soon as Aloha, Hanson, and Elvis approached the main entrance doors two pistols rattled to the sidewalk and two zombies exited through the doors with their hands and arms held above their heads.

"Is that all of you?" asked Aloha.

The two zoms nodded in unison. "Please don't freeze us," they said in stereo.

Aloha eyed the blonde one on the right. "If you're lying, and there are more of you, then you'll be frozen until the end of the next ice age. Capeesh?"

"Yes, ma'am," said the brunette zom to her left.

The fear in their eyes told Aloha they weren't lying. Her eyes narrowed. "We'll see."

Aloha handed her freeze ray to Hanson. "You stay here while Elvis and I check out the bank."

Hanson, ever the actor, nodded as he hefted the weapon. His wide mouth formed an evil grin. The two undead creatures exchanged an uneasy glance.

"OK, boys, let's go back to the deputy's pickup and lasso you two in the bed of his truck. You may not be frozen, but you're gonna be kept on ice anyway." Hanson herded them away at gunpoint. The two zoms were way past complaining.

Aloha watched them go until they disappeared around the back end of Elvis's truck. She looked into her deputy's eyes.

"I think I owe you an apology."

"About what, Sheriff?"

Aloha shrugged. "When I found you weren't shot I thought you were just being lazy for not going after the bank robbers. But after you called in you went to sleep and waited for the bad guys to surrender since they couldn't escape the force shield. Very clever; I'm impressed." Aloha frowned. "I'm sorry I misjudged you, Big E. But you have to get to bed earlier, ok?" He nodded and his cheeks flushed. She continued, "Without the force screen this situation wouldn't have ended as peacefully as it has." Since he stopped the zom's *I'm beginning to think Elvis isn't involved in the disappearances*, she thought. *There's some genius at work orchestrating these events.* A local boy's involvement didn't make sense. Elvis seemed to love the town; he didn't want to wreck the place.

Elvis's eyes flashed and his mouth became a wry smile. "It's not over yet, Sheriff."

Aloha chuckled. "True. Very true." She stepped up to the thick brass handles of the twin smoked-glass doors. She hesitated because there could be anyone or anything on the other side waiting to attack them.

Uncertainty is for the weak. She grabbed the brass handle of one of the doors and pulled it open. She had her service revolver out at the ready. If there were someone on the other side waiting in ambush she hoped she wouldn't have to shoot, but if she had to, then that was the way the monsters tumbled sometimes. If it happened to be one of Zero's henchmen who met the business end of her gun, then it wouldn't bother her in the least.

Elvis pulled the other door open. Together they stepped inside the doors, sweeping the large room for possible targets. Aloha could smell the rot left behind by the zoms.

The room was still and the air slightly stale with dust. The only sound was the echo of their leather boots on the tiled floor. To their left was a long counter with wickets for tellers. In the center of the room was a waist-high desk with racks for forms and pamphlets. It looked pretty much like any bank in any town, USA — only this one was empty. It gave Aloha a case of the creeps.

The hair on the back of her neck stood up. "Elvis, go behind the counter and check the offices against the back wall," she said, using the barrel of her pistol as a pointer. "Make sure no one's hiding under a desk."

Elvis nodded and went behind the counter through a swinging door at one end.

Aloha studied the room carefully. She spotted a piece of white paper sitting upright against the base of the table. It was only visible if you were close enough and were standing in the right position.

Aloha holstered her gun, then sank to her haunches and grabbed what she recognized was a business card. She flipped it over.

It read, *Blind Bill Barbershop. Haircuts for all at reasonable rates the whole family can afford.* The address was on Fiddler Street, and there was a phone number.

A blind barber? Now she'd heard everything.

"Sheriff!"

Elvis? Aloha drew her weapon as her body tensed. Was he in trouble? She stuffed the business card in her pants pocket and headed for the counter. She was careful to keep the bulk of her lean frame hidden by the counter.

"Elvis! You OK?" Her heart raced, and she strained to hear any sounds of a struggle or sounds that signaled her deputy was in trouble.

"Yeah…why wouldn't I be?" He appeared over the top of the counter, staring down at her. His wide face bore a mischievous grin. She'd been had.

Aloha let out the breath she'd been holding. She chuckled and stood up, re-holstering her weapon as she did.

"Elvis, one of these days I gotta instruct you on how to clear a building. Your training is sadly lacking."

"Yes, ma'am." Elvis vaulted the counter, landing on his feet next to her. "The offices are empty, and I checked the storeroom as well. Nothing appears to be out of place. The vault has been blown, and it appears some of the shelves that must have held money are empty. I'll call the bank manager and ask him for an audit to see how much is missing."

Aloha nodded. "Good thinking. I'm puzzled why zombies would need money; even the vegetarians are fed for free. And the government takes care of their day-to-day needs." She slipped her hand into her pocket and took out the barber's business card. "I did find this." She showed Elvis the business card she'd found.

Elvis visibly paled, and his eyes widened.

"Something wrong?"

Between trembling lips he said, "Blind Bill was — I mean, is, my brother's best friend."

"What does this have to do with zombie bank robbers?"

Elvis avoided her gaze by staring at the floor. His shoulders slumped. "My brother…" His voice trailed off, his words caught by emotions that looked about to overwhelm him as his eyes filled with tears.

Aloha's heart went out to him. Elvis's brother disappeared into the fourth dimension. Losing a brother in an alternate dimension could be hard on a person. But something told her it was more than his disappearance that was bothering Elvis. "What is it, Big E?" she said gently.

Elvis swallowed hard and cleared his throat. "Jerry Lee's a reformed bank robber, and Bill was his parole officer."

Chapter Fifteen

THEY ARRIVED AT BLIND BILL'S BARBERSHOP in Aloha's Huvo. The tiny car rolled to a stop in front where there was a convenient parking spot just the right size for the electric car. Of course, a larger steamer trunk would also fit between where two of Detroit's finest parked in front of and in back of her tiny transportation.

Glancing at her deputy, Aloha swallowed a laugh. Elvis was crammed into the passenger seat next to her. He looked like tuna in a can. Elvis wasn't huge, but he wasn't small either. This cupboard of a vehicle barely had room for her; passengers were definitely optional.

He was sweating, grunting, and straining to find a comfortable position against the curve of the wall next to him.

Hanson had taken Elvis's pickup truck to deliver the captured zombie bank robbers to the enclosure behind City Hall. Aloha couldn't help but be worried the enclosure was getting full. Something would have to be done soon, or the out of control zoms would eventually break out and terrorize the town. If that happened she wouldn't have much choice but to use deadly force to save the remaining residents. Her job was to keep the peace; it was in her job description.

Aloha turned the key in the ignition and assumed the engine had stopped. It was impossible to discern any difference between when the car was running versus not.

She pressed the release button, and the front of the car swung upward. She unfastened her seatbelt and got out, then walked to the front door of the barbershop. There was a sign hung on the inside of the glass door that read BACK IN 5 MINUTES. They'd have to wait.

A grunt behind her caused her to turn to face the car. Elvis had managed to release his seatbelt, but his large, muscular frame and wide shoulders were twisted into the most bizarre shape. She couldn't have hog-tied him any better.

"Need help?" she asked dryly.

"Naw, I got it." With a final grunt and a yelp of pain, Elvis managed to extract himself from the car's interior but then fell in a heap to the street in front of the car's bumper.

Untangling his intertwined limbs took him several seconds of grunting, sweating, and cursing until he was finally able to free himself from himself. Breathing hard, Elvis finally managed to struggle to unsteady feet, but he listed at an angle as if he were standing on the deck of a ship in a rolling sea.

"You OK?" Aloha asked.

"Yeah," he gasped. "I'm not riding in your car again, though." He wiped his forehead dry with a swipe of his sleeve.

Aloha grinned. "Don't blame you, big guy. I wish I had a choice."

Aloha scanned the street. There were men, women, and children coming and going from the various shops that lined Fiddler Street. A hardware store, a sewing supplies shop, a baker, butcher, fresh fruit and vegetable store, a cigar store, and video rental store made up the shopping district of Zomopolis.

As Aloha recalled the vegetarian zombie diner, Café Green, was at the end of this block.

Blind Bill's Barbershop had a sign in the window that advertised he cut hair for men, women, children, and zombies. Aloha would never have thought zom hair would grow, never mind need cutting, but the reality was most zoms were half-human. They ate, and they needed their hair cut. Certainly, they would eventually rot away, but with the new wonder drugs they could survive for years. Some people suggested the zoms were better off than most people.

Aloha smiled to herself. *Yeah, right, being undead is so much better than being alive.*

A tapping sound behind her made her turn around. A man with steel-gray hair, dark sunglasses covering his eyes, using a white cane he tapped side to side in front of him, was headed toward them. He stopped just short of them and sniffed the air.

"Hello, Sheriff, I'm Blind Bill."

Aloha glanced at Elvis.

"And the man with you is no doubt Deputy Elvis Bushwood."

"Hey, Bill, good to see ya," said her deputy.

"How do you do that?" asked Aloha.

Bill grinned. "Why don't you come into the shop, and I'll tell you."

"Sure. We have something to ask you about anyways."

"Of course. This way." Aloha and Elvis stepped back to allow Bill to move to the barbershop door where he took out a key and opened the door. A bell over the door rang brightly announcing them.

Once inside, Bill flipped the sign around to show the shop was open to passersby and then went to hang up his light spring jacket on a well-worn oak coat stand. The shop reeked of nostalgia.

Four barber chairs made of polished chrome and burnished steel with pea-green cushions was the highlight of the room. Along one wall behind the chairs was a mirror. Under the mirror was a waist-high counter inset with sinks — one for each chair — and barber's tools such as combs, electric clippers, and towels.

Along the opposite wall were four padded chairs where customers could wait their turns. In front of these stood a coffee table covered with magazines. Aloha stifled a chuckle when she saw the dates on the magazines were as much as a decade old. Elvis sat in one of the chairs and folded his hands in his lap. He appeared to have recovered from the car ride.

"You have a nice place here, Bill," Aloha said, moving to study the calendar hung on the wall over the chairs. The calendar depicted ducks of various kinds and was current. "You work alone?"

"This an interrogation, Sheriff?"

Aloha chuckled and turned to face the barber. "No, of course not. But do tell us how you were able to identify us so easily."

A sly smile came over Bill's bloodless lips. "Elementary, my dear Sheriff. You wear cinnamon perfume, Eau du Charlotte Paige, correct?"

Aloha wanted to nod, but instead she said, "Yes. What of it?"

"That brand of perfume isn't sold in Zomopolis, but is in Washington, D.C., and other large cities. In the radio interview you did with the mayor when you were sworn in as sheriff you said you'd been a detective in Washington, D.C. The scent of your perfume and your voice when you were speaking to Elvis the odds were ninety percent you were the new sheriff."

Aloha crossed her arms and her brow wrinkled slightly. This guy was good, and it concerned her. How much did he really know about her? "Impressive. What about Elvis?"

She kept her tone light so as not to arouse suspicion.

Bill chuckled, then turned around and began to wash his hands in one of the sinks. "That was much easier. I'd know the smell of the greasy kid stuff he uses in his hair from fifty paces."

Aloha cast a grin at Elvis, who shrugged. "I've been coming to this barbershop since I got my first haircut when I was three," he explained.

Bill finished washing, turned off the water, and picked up a dry towel. As he wiped his hands he turned to face Aloha. "You said you had a question for me?"

"Yes, I do. This morning we arrested a gang of zombie bank robbers at the First Zomopolis City Bank." Aloha scanned the titles of the magazines. *Field and Stream, Guns and Ammo, Famous Monsters of Film Land.* Bill had quite a collection, but nothing unusual for a barber in a town like this one. "I found your business card on the floor of the bank, as if it were a clue I was meant to find." Aloha glanced at Bill and silently cursed herself.

Bill was blind, so his eyes were hidden behind dark sunglasses.

She could read truth in the eyes. There were always signs of deception or surprise; she'd never met anyone who could hide what they were thinking completely. A suspect's eyes were her playground.

But how do you read a blind man's eyes? *Answer: you can't.*

"A lot of people have my business card. I wish I could help." The bell over the door rang, interrupting them, and a boy, who looked to be about six or seven years old, entered the shop ahead of a slender, raven-haired woman with wire-rimmed glasses perched on her long nose.

"Hello, Bill," the woman said, "Ryan needs his hair cut."

Looking the boy over Aloha had to agree. His dirty blond hair did look a little shaggy with hairs sticking up in random spikes.

The woman eyed Elvis, who offered her a tight grin. "Is there a long wait, Bill?" she asked, shifting her gaze to the blind barber.

"No, Mrs. Willington, not at all. This is the sheriff," Bill indicated Aloha by pointing an index finger at her, "and her deputy." Bill nodded at Elvis.

The woman's features scrunched as if she'd sucked on a lemon. "Really?"

Aloha frowned. *Does she have a problem with me?* Aloha decided to add a little sugar to the situation. She held out one hand and offered a friendly smile. "Hello, Mrs. Willington, my name's Aloha Armstrong, I'm the new sheriff."

Mrs. Willington tentatively took Aloha's hand in hers and gave it one limp shake that reminded Aloha of trying to grab Jell-O. *Gross.*

The boy climbed into Bill's barber chair and began to bounce up and down while giggling. "Hi, sheriff," he said gleefully. He pointed at the gun in her holster and squealed, "You ever shoot anyone?"

Aloha smiled. "Not today. At least not yet."

The boy giggled louder, but his mother scowled at Aloha disapprovingly. Ignoring the woman, Aloha signaled to Elvis it was time to go by waving one hand toward the door.

He nodded and rose from the chair. *Good, he's beginning to understand hand signals. I'll make a cop out of him if it kills me, which it better not.*

"Oh, yes, Bill, before I leave, one more question. How long were you Jerry Lee Bushwood's parole officer?"

"Six years," said Bill. "Until I retired five years ago and moved permanently to Zomopolis. I used to barber here on weekends and vacations before I retired."

130

"Have you seen Jerry Lee since?"

"That's two questions, Sheriff."

Aloha's mouth formed a smile. "Never was good at math."

Bill chuckled. "I'd see him on occasion when he came in for a haircut."

"Really? I thought you two were best friends."

Bill paused, and Aloha noted how his shoulders tensed. "We had a falling out." There was a hint of underlying anger in his voice. The fall-out must have been bad, very bad, far worse than his words suggested.

Aloha needed Intel. She had to get in touch with L.I.P.S. HQ to find out more about Blind Bill and about the Bushwood family.

It was becoming clear there was more going on here than she had first thought. A lot more.

Chapter Sixteen

B Y THE TIME ALOHA ARRIVED HOME it was after eight. She closed the front door of her condo and sank back against the painted wood door. She closed her eyes and sighed. Her entire body ached as if she'd just completed a marathon. And she hadn't run one of those in ten years.

What a day.

A sharp rap on the door made her senses suddenly alert. She didn't have any friends, and Elvis had an Elvis Presley impersonator gig at the Friday night TZC staff party. Her deputy had asked her to come, but she'd begged off explaining she was too tired to play party sheriff and schmooze like some politician. She would have to do it soon enough but not today. Besides, Elvis was just being polite because she was new to the job. He didn't really want her there.

"Who is it?" she said.

"Hanson Braddock."

Hanson? What is he doing here? "Ok," she said. "Just a minute." She unfastened her gun belt and, after taking it off, hung it up in the safe in the hall closet. She'd clean it in the morning, just as she did every morning, before she left for the station.

Like her daddy used to say, "You can never clean your weapon too much." On days like this she really missed her father. Daddy died of cancer three years ago.

After checking her appearance in the hall mirror (horrified to see her sunken eyes and stress-lined face) she fluffed her unruly red curls with her long fingers as best she could, then went to open the front door.

Hanson stood on the front stoop, a paper grocery bag brimming with produce in his arms. His rugged features were split by a smile that forced her to smile in kind.

"Hi," he said brightly. "Some day, huh?"

Aloha relaxed her shoulders. She wasn't alone in that estimation. "Yeah, some day." She cringed inside. "Where are my manners? Please come in." She stepped aside and let Hanson enter. She closed and locked the door behind him.

"Where's Sharona?" she asked.

He looked at her with a tight smile on his lips. She'd struck a nerve. "Not here. Unless you invited her?"

Aloha decided whatever his relationship with Sharona it was none of her business; she'd drop the subject. Besides the smell of onions and garlic coming from the grocery bag as he passed her made her stomach grumble, and it dawned on her she hadn't eaten anything all day. A home-cooked meal would really hit the spot right now.

"Hungry?" he asked.

She wondered if he could read minds. In her line of work she'd seen many strange things, so mind readers were not beyond the realm of possibility. But she'd thought at first Elvis could read minds, now Hanson. *I must be getting too paranoid to be normal, whatever normal is.*

"As a matter of fact, yes, very."

"Great. I brought the fixings for a spaghetti and meatball dinner for two. I'm a pretty fair cook," he said as he scanned the room visible from the entryway.

Aloha's condo had two bedrooms, one of which she used for an office. The total square footage was 1,200, very large for Zomopolis, but she was expected to entertain and "press the flesh" as part of her duties as a town official so she needed the extra space. Most single people in town were only allowed a one-bedroom. She planned to rent it until she decided if she was staying longer than the current assignment. The L.I.P.S. paid the rent through a holding company, Don't Know Jack Inc.

"Sorry about the mess." Not that she really cared. She let dirty clothes fall where she took them off until laundry day. And laundry day was tomorrow. She lived alone and hadn't had a steady boyfriend in over three years, not since she broke it off with Matt Butcher, ex-zombie. She'd gotten so used to not having guests it made her feel pathetic when she did. *Oh, well, if they don't like the way I don't clean house they can always leave.* Deep in her core she hoped Hanson would stay.

"That's OK. I'm not the neatest person either. Where's the kitchen?"

Aloha's mouth began to water at the thought of the home-cooked meal. So much for a fat-free yogurt cup and a plain rice cake for dinner. "At the end of the hall," she nodded down the hallway behind her. "Turn left when you get to the end."

"OK. I'll get started while you open the wine." He reached into the bag and pulled out a bottle of white wine, which he handed her.

"White, for Italian food?"

He grinned, and his eyes twinkled, causing her to become weak in the knees. *Get a grip, girl, it's only dinner.* "OK if we break the rules just this once? I prefer white."

She also preferred white, and this was her favorite house white. "OK," she agreed, "I won't make any arrests tonight. Besides, I'm off duty."

"Glad to hear it. I'll be in the kitchen." Hanson disappeared with his bags down the hall toward the kitchen.

Aloha watched him walk around the corner and wondered if she'd made a mistake. Having dinner with a strange man felt like a date. She didn't date. In her business, dating led to complications, and complications led to questions. Uncomfortable questions. Where did you work before you came here? Where did you go to school? What do your parents do? *Oh, well, Mr. Date, I was a spy, my parents were spies, and I went to spy school...* He'd be gone before the dessert was served.

Then again she'd met Matt on a case; then again Matt dumped her two weeks after the case was over. She didn't want to feel that kind of pain again.

"Oh, the life I lead," she muttered as she hunted for the wine opener in the sideboard next to her cluttered dining room table. The dining room and living room were actually part of one larger room. The rental company provided the furniture. Since she didn't entertain, the table had become the depository for newspapers and magazines.

She found the cheap corkscrew just as Hanson entered carrying a plate of crackers and what seemed to be duck pâté, which, from the look of it, would no doubt be perfectly spiced and smooth and creamy on her tongue. Here in the States people called it liverwurst.

She hadn't seen good pâté since her mission in Paris to capture the mad bell ringer, which of course she had. The L.I.P.S. agent always got her man, woman, monster, or hunchback.

"Duck?" she asked as she stuck the corkscrew into the bottle's cork and began to twist. She pulled out the cork with a wet pop.

"You know your fine dining," Hanson said admiringly. "Impressive."

He used his free arm to sweep the discarded clothing thrown haphazardly across the coffee table to the floor, and then set the plate on the table. "Sorry about the Ritz crackers. I couldn't find any saltines."

Aloha smiled as she selected two wine glasses from the row of glasses on top of the sideboard and set them on the coffee table next to the plate. The glasses appeared to be clean enough. "No worries."

She poured wine into each glass. Setting the bottle on the table, she picked up the two glasses and handed one to Hanson.

"What shall we toast to?" she said.

"How about to a peaceful evening?" Hanson said with a wry grin.

Aloha snorted. "Wouldn't that be nice for a change?"

~~~

Hanson's spaghetti and meatballs turned out to be as delicious as the duck pâté, but she'd only eaten half. She was too tired to eat more. She wiped the corners of her mouth with one of the hand towels she'd managed to find in the linen closet. Since she didn't have napkins the two fuchsia-colored towels were an adequate substitute.

"That was very, very good," said Aloha with a weary sigh. The meal, while excellent, when coupled with the wine, had made her sleepy.

Hanson looked up from his nearly empty dinner plate, the empathy evident in his gentle hazel eyes as he gazed at her. "Tough day at the office?"

She nodded and threw the towel on her half-eaten dinner. "Yeah. I found a business card on the floor of the bank for Blind Bill's Barbershop. We interviewed Bill." She summarized the highlights of the conversation with Bill. "I don't know if it's going to lead anywhere yet. We'll see. At least it's a clue."

"Do you think there's anything to it?" Hanson speared half a meatball with his plastic fork, raised it to his mouth, and popped it in.

Aloha shrugged. "I don't know. But Bill pointed out that anyone could have left his business card in the bank. And he's right, of course. I don't dismiss any details until I decide they aren't worth following or if they don't link to anything else. My jury's still out on Blind Bill."

"Did anything seem odd about him?"

Aloha paused to think, replaying the interview in her mind. She froze. *Hold on.* "Yeah. He pointed at me and nodded at Elvis when he introduced us to Mrs. Willington."

"Why is that odd?"

Aloha eyed her new friend. "He says he's blind, but the way he pointed made me think otherwise."

"So you think he's faking blindness?"

Aloha's insecurity surfaced. "No, not really. Elvis told me Bill's been blind for a long time. And Bill told us he could smell us, so he probably knew where to point."

Hanson's brow furrowed. "I'm sorry if I upset you it's just that I have a cousin who was blinded when he was ten, and I'm a little sensitive on the topic."

"That's not what concerns me. It means Bill was lying." Her stomach muscles tightened. "But 'why' is the question I need to answer." She looked into Hanson's gentle eyes. "Thank you, Hanson." She paused. "For everything."

He rose from his chair and picked up his plate. "Dessert?"

"No, thank you." The corners of her mouth curled up slightly. "A sheriff's gotta watch her figure." Especially when her uniform fit like a very snug glove.

~~~

Though she really, really, really wanted to kiss him goodnight properly she let him leave with nothing more than a smile, a nod, and a peck on the cheek. At least she'd have some food in her fridge since Hanson left the remainder of the groceries. Not that she'd be cooking them before they rotted, but groceries were a sign she had at least attempted to move in.

Now that she was alone she went upstairs to her bedroom and began to undress. Naked, she padded across the thick rug to the ensuite bathroom and started to draw water in the tub for a bath. A hot bath would relax her so she'd sleep better.

A loud thump from below startled her. She froze and shut off the running tap. Listening intently, she heard the unmistakable sound of breaking glass. Someone was breaking in. She padded to the bedroom door and locked it from the inside as slowly and as quietly as she could.

She caught a glimpse of herself in the mirror over the dresser. *I can't very well confront whoever it is dressed like this,* she smiled to herself, *or should I say* undressed. There wasn't time to don her discarded uniform. Sweatpants. She had two pair in the closet and t-shirts in the dresser drawer.

Moving to the closet Aloha was horrified to see it was empty except for a single dry-cleaned uniform still covered in the plastic sleeve. *Laundry day.*

Then she recalled where her sweatpants were; they were lying amongst the discarded clothing on her bathroom floor. She winced. The thump of heavy footsteps started up the stairs. She was running out of time and clean clothing.

Hurrying to her dresser she saw the t-shirts were also missing. Laundry day was tomorrow. But in the second drawer from the top she found the box containing the last gift Matt had given her.

Pulling it out, she placed the box on the top of the dresser. Removing the lid she found the shorts with the words FAT ASS in block letters emblazoned across the seat and the hand-prints painted on the matching sweatshirt as if they were gripping the curve of her breasts. *I hate this thing; it's so demeaning. I don't know why I kept it, but now I'm glad I did.* Shaking her head she hurriedly pulled on the shorts and the sweatshirt, rolling her eyes as she caught a glimpse of herself in the dresser mirror.

When Matt gave her this gift she could not believe he expected her to actually wear these things. She wasn't a prude, but it was so insulting to her as a woman she'd never bothered to put them on, until now.

There was a knock on the door, and she moved to her nightstand where she kept a stun pistol provided by Dr. Oh. One charge would knock out a 200-pound opponent for up to eight hours. She didn't wish to kill intruders because in her experience it was surprisingly difficult to question a corpse.

After checking the power gauge she was relieved to see the weapon was fully charged. At least something was going her way.

She quickly moved to the bedroom door holding the gun at the ready. There was another sharp rap on the door. Burglars and rapists didn't knock.

"Who is it?"

"Elvis," came the muffled reply.

Elvis? *Why did he break into my house?* Her anger boiled over. "Elvis! What are you doing! You scared the crap outta me!" She unlocked the door then threw it open. The door banged against the wall, leaving a deep door-handle impression in the wallboard.

Aloha sighed inwardly. *There goes the damage deposit.*

Elvis stepped back, the fear evident in his eyes. His arms windmilled as her sudden outburst threw him off balance, and he teetered on the top step of the staircase.

Aloha grabbed his right arm with both hands and yanked him toward her. He closed his eyes just before he ran face-first into the center of her chest between her breasts. Aloha released his arm and Elvis stumbled forward, his weight taking her with him. His momentum carried them both back into her bedroom where he collapsed onto the carpet with her underneath him. "Get off me!" she shouted, pounding his back with the butt of the stun pistol.

"Owww. Sorry," he said. "I'm so sorry." He scrambled off her, desperately trying to avert his gaze from the painted handprints on her chest until he finally covered his eyes with his hands. "You shore don't look like the last sheriff."

He was still dressed in his impersonator costume. *Seventies fat Elvis, puh-leaze. He looks ridiculous. White jumpsuit, sequins on everything, big hair, and sideburns halfway to his chin.*

Aloha sat up, then got to her feet. "What's the meaning of this intrusion?" she said angrily.

"Meaning?"

Aloha gritted her teeth. Looking at the stun pistol, she thought about stunning him just for good measure, but decided to wait until she heard her deputy's reasons for this home invasion. "I want the reason, Elvis. The reason you broke into my house."

He stole a peek at her between his fingers, and then closed them again. His cheeks flushed crimson. "I didn't break in."

Aloha snorted in disgust. She tossed the pistol on the bed. "Breaking glass usually spells break-in to me."

"I have a key."

Aloha stopped and stared at Elvis, who still had his eyes covered and was cowering under her verbal attack. *He has a key to my rented condominium?*

She crossed her arms. "Where did you get a key?"

"From the rental company?" he said sheepishly.

The mayor owned the rental company. Elvis was sent to spy on her. But why? What did Sharona Figer want? Or more correctly what did Sharona think she had that was worth breaking in to her house to steal?

"And the breaking glass?"

"Sorry, I had a glass of water and dropped the glass. But don't worry I'll clean it up."

"Elvis. Look at me."

Her deputy slowly uncovered his eyes. They quickly became round circles as he scanned her up and down.

Aloha stood still and waited for him to finish. But patience was not one of her virtues so she gave up after only a few seconds of his ogling.

"Seen enough?" she asked sarcastically. He nodded, his cheeks a bright red. "Good. Then we can get back to business. Why did Sharona send you to spy on me?"

"I'm not spying," he said adamantly.

"Then why are you in my house?"

His eyes shifted to the dresser, then back to her.

So, she thought, *there's something in this room he's after*. But what could it be? "Deputy," she began forcefully, her brow wrinkled, "you work for me. You better tell me what you're after or you can turn in your badge. It's up to you."

Elvis's lower lip began to tremble and his eyes filled with tears. "But, sheriff, the mayor said the same thing. I don't know what to do." He looked about to launch into a full-scale bawling session. She detested men who cried.

Nonetheless it surprised her when she actually felt sorry for him.

She knew she should fire his butt and kick him into the gutter, but she couldn't do it. He was the only deputy she had, and she hated the idea of having to hire another, given the slim pickings she'd seen in this town.

Besides she'd just started to train him, and her time and effort would go to waste. She didn't believe in needless waste. But she wasn't about to let him off easy. And of course he knew the town and the people in it far better than she did.

"Now, now, Big E, take it easy. I'm not going to fire you, provided you tell me what's going on right now."

"I really don't know, Sheriff. The mayor asked me to keep an eye on you and search your condo for anything unusual."

"Unusual? Like what?"

He shrugged. "I have no idea. It seems a little vague to me too. But the mayor said someone told her you were more than just the sheriff."

Aloha tensed. "What does that mean and did Sharona say who this someone is?"

Elvis shook his head. "I'm so sorry, Sheriff, I really wish I had more to tell you, but the mayor didn't tell me much of anything."

Aloha crossed her arms. "OK, that's all for now. But remember you work for me first; tell Sharona you didn't find anything unusual and then tell me how she reacted. We good?" He nodded and offered her a weak grin.

She smiled and patted him on the shoulder. "Why don't you go home and sleep on it, and in the morning we'll talk some more. OK?"

It seemed a little cruel to send him home without letting him off the hook, except he had invaded her space without an invitation. She knew from experience he wouldn't sleep a wink worrying all night about losing his job, and possible criminal trespass charges. Elvis was a pawn in a much larger scheme. The last thing he was was a criminal.

Of course, she wouldn't be filing any charges against him. Clearly Elvis was being manipulated, which really bugged her, but he still needed a little softening up.

A poor night's sleep seemed just the right kind of pressure to encourage her deputy to reveal whatever secrets he was keeping from her.

Elvis sighed and his shoulders drooped. "Thank you."

He turned and shuffled to the open bedroom door. Before he disappeared down the stairs, he called out, "You better put some different clothes on, Sheriff, if you're goin' out."

Aloha rolled her eyes and smirked. *No kidding.*

Chapter Seventeen

HANSON ARRIVED AT HIS ONE-BEDROOM HOUSE on Harp Road a little before eleven o'clock. The moon was full, giving his well-manicured lawn an eerie glow as if the green grass were coated with snow.

If it had been snow it would have been as fake as the moon in the sky. The army engineers that built the dome that protected Zomopolis from the outside world (Or was it, as he often thought, the other way around?) had created a simulated environment with weather, sunshine, moon and stars, or whatever the programmers deemed necessary to create the illusion of a real town with real days and real nights.

He shut off the engine and got out of his Toyota Prius.

He walked slowly up the driveway toward the cement steps leading to the front door of his house. Since he lived alone he was only allowed a single-bedroom house. Aloha was fortunate to have two bedrooms because she was the sheriff. Therefore her entitlements were part of her increased responsibility. Sheriffs were expected to host social events in their homes.

Too political a job for my tastes.

But, boy, what a slob. He couldn't believe the mess in her place.

Before he started cooking he had to clean out her refrigerator. There were a few things not even he could identify. He was glad he'd found a pair of rubber gloves and a set of tongs. He wasn't about to contract some deadly food borne disease as part of his investigation. He couldn't help his father if he was dead, now could he?

Arriving at his front door, Hanson took out his house key and let himself in.

What frustrated him more than anything was so far he hadn't discovered any clues as to whether his father was alive or dead. He had hoped by helping Aloha with her investigation he'd be closer to solving the mystery of his father's disappearance. So far he'd learned zip.

But there was something about Aloha that intrigued him. Besides being beautiful, she was smart and fearless. He admired her courage under fire and her resourcefulness. He hoped she didn't think his making dinner for them was a date. He didn't need any romantic entanglements right now.

He flicked the light switch on the wall next to the front door but nothing happened. He scowled. No doubt a fuse had blown again. The house was sixty years old, and the electrical system had never been upgraded. The fuses were larger versions of the ones used in cars at one time. He kept replacement fuses in the garage.

Since he was tired he considered waiting until morning when it was light to replace the fuse but decided he better do it now. He had milk in the refrigerator that might go bad by morning.

Without locking the door he closed it and headed for the garage. Once there he tried the switch on the wall, but again nothing happened.

Great. This meant the main fuse had blown. Now he had to find the flashlight in the dark.

He sighed and began to feel his way along the wall until his fingers came into contact with the workbench a few feet from the door. The flashlight was across the darkened garage.

He felt along the workbench until he was sure the flashlight should be directly in front of him. He reached out and felt the cold steel of an empty hook. He frowned. Now where could it be?

"Don't move, Mr. Braddock," said a mechanically enhanced voice. "I have a gun trained on your head, and I will not hesitate to shoot, so don't test me."

Suddenly he was blinded when a beam of light flicked on directed into his eyes. Instinctively Hanson held out one hand to block the bright light. His eyes immediately began to water, and he blinked trying in vain to get a look at the intruder.

"What do you want?" he gasped.

"I have a message for Aloha Armstrong."

"What does that have to do with me? I own a diner. I'm a cook, not a cop."

The voice emitted a harsh mechanical laugh. "I've been watching you, Mr. Braddock, and I beg to differ. You have skills far beyond that of a mere cook."

Hanson blinked repeatedly as his sight began to adjust. He thought he could make out a shrouded figure holding the flashlight. Whoever it was wasn't very tall. The distinct odor of bubble gum wafted over him. Could his captor be a kid? Though he sure didn't talk like a kid, at least not like any he'd ever met.

"What's the message?" said Hanson, deciding to get this over with as quickly as possible.

"Tell Sheriff Armstrong she needs to go back to TZC. The solution she seeks is there."

"Solution? What solution? And to what?"

Did he mean a solution to a mystery or a solution as in liquid? Zombie Away was a liquid, as was the beer they manufactured. Hanson hated riddles. "I don't understand."

"That is all I can say." The light suddenly went out, and the garage was once again plunged into inky darkness.

"Great," muttered Hanson. "Just great."

He reached out and touched the edge of the workbench and made his way back to the door. Just as he got there the light in the garage and the porch light over the kitchen door came on. The good news: the power was back on; the bad news: he was blinded again.

Hanson closed his eyes tight and uttered an oath of frustration. He was tired of this game.

The echo of a car engine starting came from down the street out front of his house. Hanson blinked to try to clear his bleary vision.

Without waiting for fear he'd lose his opportunity to catch his assailant, he broke into a run, first to his driveway, then into the street. Once there he paused to scan for the source of the engine. He spotted a single-passenger car. He arrived in time to see headlights on the tiny car snap on. He broke into a run, hoping to catch sight of the driver.

The car made a quick U-turn, and then sped away. Hanson gritted his teeth and willed his legs to go faster, but still the little car was putting distance between them. Soon it turned the corner at Xylophone Avenue and disappeared. Breathing hard Hanson arrived at the corner. He stopped and bent forward at the waist placing his hands on his thighs and gulping in as much air as he could. He watched the red taillights receding into the distance until they became the size of fireflies before disappearing altogether.

As he regained his breath and his heart rate slowed, Hanson stood up straight and slapped the side of his thigh.

The car had gotten away, and he hadn't even gotten a glimpse of the driver.

He walked back toward his house muttering to himself about not having had the foresight to focus on the tiny car's license plate. In fact, he wasn't even certain it had one. *I must be in the land of missed opportunities*, he mused.

Upon arriving back at his front door he went inside and sat on the soft brown leather sofa in the living room. He wondered who he should call since he'd had a break-in. It didn't feel right to call Aloha so soon. He'd give her the message in the morning.

Elvis? Should he call the deputy? His lips pursed. He'd call Elvis. Hanson rose from the sofa and walked to the kitchen. A wireless telephone sat on the counter near the toaster. The kitchen, like his living room, was neat and organized. The kitchen smelled of lemon cleanser.

He hated lying to Aloha by telling her he was a slob too, but he had to win her confidence if he was going to find his father.

He snatched the phone out of the charger and dialed 911. In the evening hours, when Aloha was off duty, the town's emergency phone system was call-forwarded to Elvis. He'd call the volunteer fire chief or the hospital if they were needed. There were two rings, and then Elvis spoke, "Hello?" The background noise told Hanson the deputy was in his truck.

Hanson smiled to himself. Aloha was right about his lack of training.

"Hi, Elvis. It's Hanson. There's been a break in."

"Yeah, I know."

Surprise registered on Hanson's face. "How do you know so soon?"

"Well, I was there, wasn't I?" Elvis said sarcastically.

What is he talking about? But you may as well argue with the wind as with a crazy person. "OK, fine. Can you come over right away?"

"Why?"

"There's been a break-in."

Elvis snorted, and his tone became angry. "Like I said I *know* already. Do we have to keep talkin' about it? It's kinda embarrassing, ya know."

Hanson felt himself growing impatient. "Listen, Deputy, someone broke into my house and threatened me with a gun." (He didn't know for sure they had a gun but he or she said they did, which was good enough for him.)

The tone in Elvis's voice changed. "You had one, too? Man, it's as if there's been an epidemic of break-ins lately." The annoyance in the deputy's voice returned. "Why did you have to embarrass me? Why didn't you tell me instead of wasting my time and letting me ramble on?"

Hanson rolled his eyes. *Oh, brother.* "Huh, sorry, now can you come over to my place right away?"

"Sure. Give me the address." Hanson told him the address. "I'll be there in ten minutes." Then Elvis hung up.

Hanson replaced the phone in the charger. Now he wondered where the other break-in had occurred. He dismissed a fleeting thought it might involve Aloha. If there was one thing he was certain of it was that the Woman from L.I.P.S. could more than take care of herself. An intruder would have his hands and arms full with Aloha Armstrong.

Chapter Eighteen

A LOHA STOOD IN THE WINDOW of her bedroom gazing over the sunlit weed-infested back yard. What grass hadn't been chocked out by dandelions, crabgrass, and chickweed had gone to seed.

One day she'd cut and weed the yard, but not today. Today she had reports to finish.

Her mind was fresh and alert from a good night's sleep, and she'd even done a load of laundry. After the events of last night she would keep a clean pair of sweatpants in her closet at all times, and at least one clean t-shirt in her dresser drawer. She wasn't about to be caught with her pants down ever again.

The disgusting shorts and sweatshirt were now in the trashcan in the alley. She'd finally cleaned out her mental house. Matt Butcher was now part of history, gone forever from her life. Today would be her day to start again. And if she wanted to go out with Hanson Braddock, then she would.

She padded into the kitchen pleased to see the automatic coffee machine had finished bubbling and spitting steam. The room was filled with the smell of the fresh roasted beans she'd ground moments before.

After taking a large coffee cup from the cupboard above the counter next to the stove, she poured a cup of the fresh brew. She took her first sip, sighed, and closed her eyes as the roasted flavor of the beans tinged with chocolate and floral accents flowed across her taste buds. "Yum-yum," she breathed. "Can I make a good cuppa or what?"

The telephone rang. She set the cup on the counter. Before she started the laundry she'd put in a call to the L.I.P.S Intelligence Division. That was an hour ago so it surprised her they were calling back so soon. She'd anticipated it taking a week for them to get back to her.

She plucked the receiver from the charger; the number on call display was L.I.P.S., all right. Aloha thumbed the answer button and brought the phone to her ear.

"Hi, Wally?"

Wally Hansberger was her contact in Intel. He had a crush on her, and he was sweet. But she swore to herself to never abuse their friendship. Having a friend in Intel had advantages, like now, when he called her back so soon.

"It's Simon, Agent Armstrong."

Oh, oh, it was Simon Mynass, director of L.I.P.S. *Now I'm in trouble.*

He never called her in the middle of a mission. Though she knew he couldn't see her, Aloha instinctively threw back her shoulders and straightened her posture.

"Uhhh, hello, sir…I mean, Director, sir."

Simon chuckled, sending a wave of relief through her. *My ass is not freshly mowed grass yet.*

"Don't worry, Aloha, you're not in trouble. Wally gave me the intelligence you asked for. He said I better see it before he sent it you. He's sending the file by encrypted e-mail as we speak, but I thought I'd call before you read the file to warn you."

Warn me? "Yes, sir, what's the problem?"

The director paused, causing Aloha's heart rate to rise. "This may be the biggest threat we've ever faced. The fate of the country, maybe even the world, is at stake this time."

"Yes, sir?"

"We believe someone is planning to let the zombies loose to wreck havoc and to overthrow the government of the United States. And we believe this is only phase one of a larger operation. Once the U.S. is under their control, whoever is behind this heinous plot plans to use zombies to conquer the rest of the planet and appoint themselves Emperor."

Aloha's brow wrinkled and her stomach muscles tightened. "Is it the B.U.T.T.S., sir?'

"Yes, at least we believe so." The director paused again. *Here comes the tough part, my new mission objective.* "Aloha, as difficult it is for me to say, you will find a red stake in the file. You *know* what that means."

Aloha's eyes widened, and her jaw clenched. "Yes, sir, I do."

A red stake meant she had to assassinate someone. She'd dreaded this day since she first heard of red stakes in her academy days; now it was her turn.

A sanctioned assassination order had been called a red stake since Operation Red Stake forty years ago when a particularly nasty vampire had to be taken out by a L.I.P.S. operative.

The L.I.P.S. operatives death had been particularly ugly because another agent had to stake him through the heart after he turned into an undead monster.

There had only been four red stakes issued in the intervening decades since that first order was issued, and in every instance the agent died in the line of duty.

No agent wanted to be assigned a red stake order, but Aloha steeled herself and tried to swallow. Unfortunately her mouth was too dry so she licked her lips before speaking. "Who is the target, sir?"

There was a rustling of papers on the other end of the line, and then the director cleared his throat. "Hanson Braddock."

~~~

Aloha stood still as a statue, but her hands were trembling. She felt faint but managed to maintain her composure. She was a professional agent. No matter what feelings she had for Hanson, he was now the target. For the first time in her career she would have to assassinate someone.

No, she corrected herself, not just someone, Hanson Braddock, to be exact. It seemed hard to believe Hanson was a B.U.T.T.S. agent working to unleash a zombie horde on the world, but the Intel in the file said he was an enemy agent, so he had to be.

The problem was she'd had a meal with the man, and what was more, she liked him. Not that she had never shared a meal with the odd bad guy who wanted to take over the world before, but those meals were usually poisoned so she usually left hungry.

Sure she'd killed her share of bad guys in the line of duty, but that was all part of being an agent.

Bad guys falling into flaming pits of oil or being impaled on steel fences or killed by explosions when their secret bases hidden inside hollowed-out volcanoes self destructed or when they drowned in pudding — all perfectly normal ends for bad guys. But assassination? This wasn't going to be a walk on easy street.

She steeled herself and set her jaw. While it wasn't normal operational practice, she had to know why, if she were going to assassinate a man she had grown fond of, and who had saved her life more than once, she had to confirm the Intel.

"Uhhh, sir, I have to know the reason for the red stake. And not just what's in the file." She'd seen enough briefing files to know they were usually highlights, often skipping over many important details. She sensed this operation was far more complex than a normal operation.

Simon cleared his throat. Aloha sensed he was nervous. "I will send you a second encrypted e-mail, Agent Armstrong. The full details will be in the second file. Every piece of Intel we have on Braddock." He paused, and she felt as if the second shoe were about to drop (she hoped it would be a stylish heel with a fun pattern, but since the director was a man it was probably an oxford casual). "The file is large, very large."

"Sir? How large?"

"Five thousand pages. It will take some time to download, so be prepared to be patient."

"Yes, sir. Do I have permission to read the full file before I complete the red stake order?"

There was another lengthy pause, during which Aloha expected the director to say no, until he finally responded. "Yes."

He lowered his voice, and his tone became deadly serious. "No agent has ever disobeyed a red stake order. I expect you to follow yours. I'm trusting you, Aloha."

Aloha's heart sank. She knew she had to obey orders regardless of what she found in the file. Hanson Braddock would die by her hand. She said, "I know, sir, I won't let you down." *But only if the Intel checks out.* With that, she cut the connection by pressing the off button on her phone.

Aloha refilled her coffee mug, then she went upstairs to the second bedroom. She closed the door behind her and engaged the hidden locking mechanism.

The wall containing the door slid to the left into a slot that couldn't be seen unless you knew what to look for. Where the door and doorframe had been was now a blank wall made of plasti-steel.

The lights in the room changed from plain white to a soft red glow, and the four-drawer dresser against the far wall split in half, both halves folding back to reveal a 32" flat screen monitor attached to the wall and a keyboard on a built-in desk. A panel in the floor slid aside and a chair that appeared to be made of shiny plastic locked into place in front of the desk.

Aloha strolled over to the desk while taking a sip from her cup and sat on the chair. She sighed as the chair molded to her, supporting her in all the right places, and the warm coffee flowed across her tongue.

There was nothing better than a great mug of coffee. And Dr. Oh made the best furniture in which to enjoy a good cuppa ever.

"Wish that chair was me," said a young man's voice from hidden speakers on either side of the monitor.

Aloha smiled to herself. The doc had programmed Wally's voice and personality into the computer interface.

The computer sounded and acted like the lovable nerd. Wally had a crush on her, and she liked him, but he just wasn't her type.

She rolled her eyes. Not that she'd made great choices in men in the past. *Imagine my surprise when I fell for a half-zombie, now a B.U.T.T.S. agent. Boy, can I pick 'em or what?*

"I appreciate the compliment, Wally, but I need to see my e-mail. Can you bring it up please?"

"Certainly, Agent Armstrong, right away."

Aloha took another sip of her coffee using the mug to hide her amused smile. No matter how many times she told the computer to call her Aloha it never did. Obviously, the doc had programmed familiarity out of the machine.

It amused her Dr. Oh felt the need to protect her virtue. That ship had sailed a long time ago. She sighed under her breath. What could have been, she thought wistfully.

The e-mail icon clicked in the tray at the bottom of the monitor and the e-mail user id and password screen opened. The Wally interface wouldn't be able to enter her id and password. This was what the keyboard was for.

Aloha set her mug next to the keyboard and entered *agent 111* in the user id field and *catlove33* in the password field and then tapped enter with her index finger.

The screen went white, and then the flaming L.I.P.S. logo appeared, quickly followed by a list of her e-mails. There were two new ones, both from Simon. She opened the one with the earlier time stamp first. There was a file attached.

She clicked on the attachment icon, which engaged the encryption software. The software scanned the file, and then a password dialogue box appeared. Aloha keyed in her secret number and then hit enter.

The file icon opened, and the document opened. She scanned the first page and quickly realized it was a secret document, one that could only be shared with other enforcement agencies, such as local and state police departments, and the lower security level FBI agents at regional offices.

Her eyes narrowed, and she began to read through the document. She stopped when she found the relevant part about Hanson she'd been looking for. Apparently, his father was sheriff of Zomopolis before her. In fact, his father was her predecessor, the man she was here to find or rescue, as the case warranted.

Aloha leaned back in her chair and lifted the mug to her lips once again. She took a sip and almost spat it out when she discovered her coffee had grown cold. *Yuck.* Cold coffee was the worst. She went to the bathroom and poured the rest down the sink.

"Now where was I?" she muttered once she was comfy in her chair.

"About to wonder why Hanson has a different surname than his father," offered the Wally interface.

"Yes, Wally, that's true, but how do you know?"

"The file has secret clearance, and since I'm cleared to read those designated files, I did. I like reading."

Aloha eyed the computer. The interface sounded almost proud of itself. *But it's a machine; machines don't have feelings.* She wondered if Dr. Oh had done too a good a job on virtual Wally.

"Well then, Wally, perhaps you will explain why Hanson and his father don't share the same family name."

"It's simple, really," said Wally, sounding ridiculously pleased with itself. She made mental note to contact the doc and find out if Wally-the-interface's actions were normal. Well, normal for a super-brain computer.

"Your predecessor, Sheriff Bradley, had two wives, each living in different cities. With wife number-one, his name wasn't Bradley; it was Braddock. With wife number two, he was Bradley, Sheriff of Zomopolis."

This was a surprise. "So what did he do as Braddock?"

"Made babies?"

Aloha's eyes narrowed, and she fought the urge to laugh. Instead she eased back in her chair and crossed her arms. She needed time to think.

Braddock was a son of the sheriff she was supposed to find. Somehow TZC was involved, and then there was the Zero factor. But how was Arnold Zero involved? And how was the B.U.T.T.S. involved? Did Zero work for the B.U.T.T.S. now? It was hard to imagine him as a joiner of anything. Most megalomaniacs worked alone. They usually killed their henchmen with exploding volcanoes and imploding secret underground lairs.

She blew air through her nose and sighed. She wasn't going to assassinate Hanson, that much she knew for certain. She'd been a professional agent for too many years to be fooled. Hanson was not a professional agent.

Even if the Intel file said he worked for the B.U.T.T.S. someone had screwed up, because the diner owner had no spy skills whatsoever. Even when he was under fire it was clear he had no experience with guns and gunfire. That much was clear from his actions during the bank robbery.

He did know how to fight with his fists, but with his muscular physique (*be careful where this is going, girl*, she cautioned herself) he could certainly handle himself physically. Actually more than handle himself.

She wondered if he was a cop or maybe a soldier. But cops and soldiers receive firearms training so that didn't make sense. He didn't seem comfortable with guns. Then again he could have been acting.

She recalled when she walked in on him posing for the portrait in the mayor's office. Her cheeks grew warm. She pushed away the image of his muscular bare chest and sexy sly smile.

She felt the need to talk to him. Her feelings for him had grown surprisingly fast. In fact her feelings had grown so fast it scared her.

Normally she'd have a cooling-off period and not see a man she was interested in for a few weeks, but in these circumstances she had no choice; she had to see him; she couldn't avoid him, no matter what. None of this made sense, and until it did she wasn't about to kill him.

She wouldn't assassinate him; instead she'd protect him. If word got back to Simon she hadn't killed him within a couple of days, the director would send some freelance hitters to take care of the job; he'd been known to do that when an agent wasn't in position to stop a villain. Her eyes narrowed, and she placed her elbows on the chair arms and steepled her hands, interlocking her long fingers.

Whoever Simon would send would be good, very good. It would take all her skill to stop him, or her. And stop the hired gun she would, even if it meant killing the assassin. She estimated she had two days at best before the hired gun arrived in town.

Chapter Nineteen

Hanson opened the front door after looking out the peephole at Elvis standing looking impatient, his thick arms crossed and a scowl on his face.

Someone isn't a happy camper.

"Hi, Elvis."

The deputy didn't respond as he shoved past Hanson and walked toward the hall. He issued an exclamation of satisfaction when he found the washroom halfway down the hall.

He went in and slammed the door shut behind him.

"Nice to see you, too," Hanson muttered. He closed the front door, then entered the living room, sat on the sofa, and waited for the deputy.

He glanced at his watch. He wasn't going to get a lot of sleep tonight. After ten minutes he began to wonder what the delay was. He dismissed a passing thought that Elvis might be sick. The deputy had looked fine when he entered the bathroom.

Glancing at his watch, he realized it had been at least twenty minutes now. He let out a breath then stood as his brow wrinkled with annoyance. He had to get *some* sleep tonight.

He entered the hallway and walked to the bathroom door. The light in the hall was off, so he could clearly see a sliver of light coming from under the door.

He stopped outside the door and held his breath so he could listen intently in the silence. Silence.

He pressed his right ear to the door. He heard a familiar sound. Someone was snoring softly. Hanson felt a knot of anger forming in the pit of his stomach.

He's sleeping? Hanson took a step away from the door and pounded on it with his fist. A startled yelp came from the other side of the door

"In a minute," came the rough reply.

"Out now!" Hanson said, his tone angry. He pounded on the door two more times to punctuate his words.

"Ok. OK. Take it easy," came the reply.

The door flew open and a red-faced Elvis appeared. He was doing up his belt buckle, and his shirt was only half tucked into his pants; the other half was hanging over the side of his pants. "A guy's gotta go when —"

"I know, I know...when a guy's gotta go," finished Hanson. "But you were sleeping in there, and my life's been threatened." Hanson's hands formed fists at his sides, cracking his knuckles as they tightened. He glared at the disheveled deputy.

"OK, OK, don't blow a gasket, man." He held up his hands in mock surrender.

Elvis started down the hall with Hanson following close behind him. "Ya got sumthin' to eat?" He glanced over his shoulder, and when he saw the expression on Hanson's face his normally ruddy cheeks paled and his eyes widened. "No food, huh?"

Hanson shook his head slowly.

Elvis shrugged. "OK. No worries." They entered the living room where Elvis scanned the room. He whistled softly. "Wow, nice man cave." He walked to the sofa and sat down, then ran one hand over the cushion. "Real leather. Nice."

Hanson crossed his muscular arms over his broad chest and leaned against the wall. He stared at the deputy who had snatched the television remote off the coffee table, where he'd dropped it, and turned on the television. On the screen was one of the late-night talk shows, the one with the Scottish guy.

Hanson shook his head in disgust. What kind of a cop was this guy? "Obviously a bad one," he muttered under his breath. "I should have called Aloha," he said loud enough for Elvis to hear him.

Elvis looked at him, his brow wrinkled. "Naw, you don't need her. I'm perfectly capable of taking care of all your policing needs."

Hanson snorted, uncrossed his arms, and moved to sit in his La-Z-Boy that faced the television. What was the use? "OK then, deputy, why don't you turn off the TV so I can tell you what happened."

"Why? What happened?"

"Have you been listening to anything I've been saying?" Hanson grimaced and shuffled forward so he was near the front edge of the La-Z-Boy. "Turn off the TV."

Elvis shrugged and did as Hanson asked, then turned to face Hanson, locking eyes with him. "So tell me, what happened?"

The deputy didn't take out a notebook, but Hanson didn't care anymore. He explained how he'd found the lights out when he got home.

(He left out the part about making dinner for Aloha, concerned Elvis might get the idea it was a date.) Not *might*, he thought, he *would* get the wrong idea.

If someone told him they'd made dinner for a beautiful woman he knew he'd certainly think it was a date.

After finishing with the description of his attacker Hanson watched Elvis yawn. He rolled his eyes and then said, "You do realize he or she or it had the drop on me, right?" Elvis shook his head then stretched his arms above his head. "I hope I'm not interrupting your beauty sleep?" Hanson said, his voice dripping with sarcasm.

"As a matter of fact...." Elvis started to say and then stopped when he saw Hanson's features darken, his eyes narrow, and his jaw tighten. "Never mind. So did this perp steal anything?"

Hanson thought for a second. The deputy was right. He hadn't checked the house to see if anything was missing. "I don't know. We should check, I guess."

Hanson, with Elvis close behind, walked to the hallway and opened the door that led to the upstairs. They climbed the short flight of stairs and entered his bedroom. Hanson came to a sudden stop when he saw the room had been tossed. The dresser drawers were open, the contents scattered across the hardwood floor. The night table next to the bed had been thrown on its side, the mattress lay half off the bed frame, and the covers were on the floor.

Hanson knew someone had been looking for the documents on the thumb drive where he'd copied the official FBI files concerning his father's disappearance. The information in that file was important to his investigation. Hanson had taken a night janitor job to secure the thumb drive with the information, and he wasn't about to let some thief steal it this easily.

The thumb drive was hidden in a safe place just in case this exact thing happened.

"I'm going to get my fingerprint kit," said Elvis as he turned to leave.

Hanson grabbed Elvis by the arm and stopped him before he walked out the bedroom door. "Hold on, Deputy, you won't need your fingerprint kit."

Elvis scowled and yanked his arm free. He rubbed the spot where Hanson grabbed him. "Listen, at the scene of a break-in it's standard police procedure to dust for prints. Don't you watch cop shows?"

Hanson offered the deputy a tight smile. "No, actually."

Elvis's features went slack. "Oh. Don't watch TV much, huh?"

Hanson shook his head. "Sports and news."

"Oh. Well, anyway, it's standard procedure, and I have to dust the room. The sheriff'll kill me if I don't."

Hanson crossed his arms over his chest. "The thief left a note." Hanson nodded toward the mirror above the dresser opposite the bed. Taped to the mirror was a piece of pink paper. Along the top edge of the paper in neon-blue letters were the words, FROM THE DESK OF THE SHERIFF. The message read: WE KNOW YOUR SECRET.

Elvis's jaw went slack, and he gaped at the note. His eyes gradually widened, and he looked at Hanson, whose features were marred now by a deep frown. His eyes had narrowed and were hard as coal.

"I think Sheriff Armstrong has some 'splainin' to do," said Hanson, his voice coarse and strained with pent-up rage.

Elvis scratched his scalp, and his face screwed up. "Yeah, I guess so."

Chapter Twenty

A T PRECISELY TEN O'CLOCK in the morning Aloha entered through the twin glass doors of the Sheriff's station to find Hanson and Elvis sitting behind Elvis's desk beside each other. They were engrossed in a heated conversation but dropped into silence the moment she walked into the office.

They both glared at her, their brows wrinkled, and their hard stares bored into her as if she were a mass murderer. Aloha wondered what had gotten into them.

"Hey, guys, what's up?" Aloha had brought her travel mug with her from her car. She headed to the coffee machine next to an army of green filing cabinets lining the wall to the left of the coffee station and refilled her mug. She sniffed the air. Surprisingly the coffee smelled fresh. Most days it reminded her of old burnt tar.

Big E was notorious for leaving the carafe nearly empty, forcing the next person to have to make a fresh pot if they wanted a cup.

As she turned, Aloha raised the mug of hot coffee to her lips. And took a careful sip.

She turned around slowly blowing on the hot liquid to cool it off, and froze when she saw the angry stares being directed at her. "Guys? Is something wrong?"

Hanson stood with his arms folded, his swarthy features marred by narrow angry eyes and a furrowed brow. Though he looked even better angry (as if that were possible) she didn't care for the *attitude* coming at her.

If in the future they were going to be in a relationship beyond friendship this would be the perfect precursor to their first fight, and of course she needed to keep him from dying. *Good,* she thought, *at least our first fight is out of the way.*

Too many times in the past the first fight was the last before she got dumped. Odd. She'd just realized she was always the *dumpee,* never the *dumper.*

That's just weird, she thought, I'm hot, smart—and I'm messy, but then no one's perfect, are they? True, I can kill a man in twenty-one different ways without breaking a sweat, and I have an arsenal of spy gadgets and weapons. So, what's not to love?

"Well, guys, what's going on?" She chuckled. "You two look as if you just came from a funeral."

Hanson dropped his arms to his sides and then stuffed his hands in the pockets of his jeans. He took two steps toward her. Aloha felt something emanating from him she'd never felt before. He was angry. At her. Very angry.

What have I done?

Hanson pulled out a piece of paper from his right pocket, which he handed to her. Aloha set her coffee mug on the coffee station next to the coffee machine then read the note. Her eyes went wide.

"Please explain what you think you know about me?" said Hanson his voice low and deep.

What was she going to say? Her eyes flitted from the note to lock with his. She couldn't tell him she had been ordered to kill him. Then it dawned on her. "Huh, I've never seen that note before."

She grinned. "A fact I can prove."

She turned and walked away headed to her private office at the rear of the squad room. Not that there was a squad; she and Big E were the whole enchilada of the Zomopolis Sherriff's Department.

She counted to three, and then she heard the thump of Hanson's footfalls on the carpet behind her. She smiled to herself.

Girl, you are so good at laying the bait for a man. If only she could land the ones she didn't have to throw back because they were too stupid or too arrogant or too dangerous.

She dropped into her leather executive chair and set her crossed legs on top of her desk. Her leather spike-heeled boots gleamed. How she loved these boots.

Hanson slammed the door, cutting off Elvis, who was protesting he was being left out of the explanation. Aloha sympathized with him. "Big E, go find Blind Bill and hold him for questioning. Got it?"

"Yeah, I got it," came the muffled none-too happy reply through the door.

She understood how he felt it was in one of those old detective movies on the late, late show when your cable goes out just as the murderer was about to be revealed. "And the murderer is—"

Man, do I hate when that happens.

Hanson sat in one of the two chairs on the other side of her desk. "OK. Prove it."

The uncertain edge in his voice told her he wanted to be wrong. Aloha offered him a crooked, reassuring smile. She slid open the drawer in her desk and took out a note pad, identical to the one Hanson showed her, and a pencil.

"What would you like me to write?" she said.

"Use the same wording as the note."

Aloha nodded appreciatively. Smart. *Note to self: never underestimate diner owners.* She wrote down the exact words written on the note Hanson handed her, then handed the pad of paper to him.

Hanson read it and frowned. "You did that on purpose."

She shook her head and chuckled. "Nope, sorry, I was awarded first prize for the worst handwriting by the American Medical Association."

He grinned, causing her to laugh. He opened his mouth to speak, but she stopped him by holding up one hand, then continued, "Just kidding. But I never did get a pen for mastering handwriting in the third grade like all the other kids. My handwriting has never been good."

Hanson snorted. "Good? This is the worst I've ever seen." His features relaxed, and his shoulders sagged slightly. "Sorry, but can you please write one more just so I can be sure."

It was Aloha's turn now. "I could throw you out of my office instead, you know."

Hanson shrugged. "Yeah, but indulge me anyway? Please?" He handed her the pad of paper again.

"OK." Aloha accepted the pad and wrote something, then handed it back to him.

He read it and shook his head, then ginned at her. "What does it say?"

Aloha smiled. "It says you're buying lunch."

"I am?"

"Yes." Her eyes and her tone shifted her demeanor to serious. "You and I need to talk about *secrets.* Mine and yours."

~~~

Joe's Family Diner was busy.

They served a great breakfast, but Aloha had only a cup of black coffee on the diner table in front of her. Hanson had a glass of freshly squeezed orange juice in front of him.

Aloha raised the cup and took a sip, then set the cup on the saucer with a soft clink of porcelain.

"So what secrets do you think I have?" Hanson asked. His arms rested on the table on either side of the glass, his hands flat on the table. His eyes studied hers.

Aloha frowned. "Well, for one thing you're the son of my predecessor."

Hanson visibly stiffened. "I knew you'd discover that at some point. That's not a secret."

"Well, then why didn't you volunteer the information when we met?"

Hanson averted his gaze and shrugged. "Need to know. And you didn't need to know."

Aloha scooted forward on the leatherette bench seat and leaned forward onto her elbows. "Listen, I know you came here to find out what happened to your father, so you and I have the same objective."

Hanson's eyes went wide. "Why would you be interested in what happened to my father?"

"Because we believe he knew something about a plot to release the zombies."

Hanson leaned closer, and his eyes locked on hers. Aloha could smell the musky soap he used. *Control, girl. Control.*

"Who is *we* exactly?" he said.

Aloha eased back and glanced around them. Since they'd been seated the breakfast crowd had thinned considerably, but old man McDok sat in the booth across from theirs trying to appear as if he weren't listening.

But Aloha knew the old man was drinking in their every word. She turned in the booth to face the man.

"Mr. McDok, this is designated Secret, eyes and ears only." She paused to grip her pistol in its holster. "If you hear things you're not supposed to, then I *will* have to kill you." She nailed him with a glare and forced her mouth into a thin line.

McDok stared at her, his mouth hanging open. "Really? Wow. Real black ops stuff, huh. I knew you two were secret government types the moment I laid eyes on you."

Aloha scooted along the bench seat of the booth and made a point of flicking off the safety strap of her pistol with a loud snap.

"You leaving?" she said with as much menace in her tone as she could muster.

McDok chuckled with the glee normally shown by excited 9-year-olds and slid out of the booth. "No need to shoot, Sheriff, if you really are the sheriff." He winked at her. "Mum's the word. I'll never tell anyone about you two. You can depend on me." He saluted, and then headed off with his chest thrown out.

Aloha pressed the button on the pistol's safety strap. She then turned back in the seat to face Hanson and smiled.

Hanson whistled softly under his breath. "Impressive."

"Now where were we?" Aloha paused. "Ah, yes, you want to know who I am." She looked him directly in the eyes, wanting to assure him she was being honest with him. For some reason it was important to her that he trust her. Now she was worried. Her heart pounded hard. She realized she was in love for the first time in a long time, a dangerous experience if her past rocky relationships were any measure. *Oh, crap.*

"Hanson, I'm going to violate my orders and put you at risk. Are you OK with that?" He nodded.

Aloha sighed. "I know Sharona told you I used to be a federal agent, but she didn't give you all the details." Again he nodded. She eyed him carefully. "What I'm going to tell you is top secret. You must never reveal this information to anyone." He nodded again as she took in a deep breath then continued. "I'm actually an international agent for a secret organization that dates back to the time of the crusades. We're called the Legal Investigative Protection Service known by the acronym L.I.P.S. An enemy spy organization has been our nemesis since the organization began. They are called the Big Underground Terror and Tyranny Society or the B.U.T.T.S."

Hanson gazed at her with calm, steady eyes, his expression unreadable. "Hanson," Aloha said slowly. "You and I are going to have to learn to be truthful with each other."

"And why is that?"

Oh, boy, here comes the bombshell, thought Aloha. I hope he can handle it. "Because my organization thinks you're a B.U.T.T.S. agent, and if you are, my assignment is to liquidate you."

Hanson's face sagged, and he dropped his arm off the back of the booth.

"*Liquidate* means kill, right?"

She nodded.

"Me? For what?"

"As I said, you are an enemy agent who works for an evil organization intent on taking over the world. My job is stopping you from unleashing the zombies in Zomopolis on the world, even if it's an alternate dimension. The L.I.P.S. authority extends everywhere and into every dimension. If my stopping you means assassination, then so be it." Aloha shrugged. "Someone thinks you're the linchpin to the operation so you have to be taken out."

"But I'm not an enemy agent. I've never heard of this bottoms group."

"It's the B.U.T.T.S., and they're not a group, or an after-school club; they're vicious killers, and my job is stop them." She averted her gaze. "Truthfully I've never had an assassination order before, and I'm violating my orders by not killing you right now, right here."

She turned back to face him in time to see Hanson's broad shoulders droop. He was going to complete the puzzle she'd had in her head about him since the day she'd met him.

"All right. I'll tell you what's going on."

"Go ahead. I'm listening."

~~~

For the next thirty minutes Aloha learned more than she had in the entire time since she'd taken the job as sheriff of Zomopolis. And it became clear Sharona had been hiding a lot from her.

After this crisis is over she and I are going to have a long talk.

As she suspected, Blind Bill wasn't blind, (yes, he had confirmed Bill really was a barber. At least that much was true) was employed by TZC in some secret capacity. And she suspected someone inside TZC was behind the plot to destroy the fourth wall and unleash the zombies on the world once again.

"So what did you hope to accomplish by yourself?" Aloha asked a red-faced Hanson. By the way he clenched his fists and the vein in his neck throbbed he was evidently angry about how his efforts had gone so far.

Great, she thought, *not only do I have an upset deputy who has lost his brother to that wall, but now my potential friend, Hanson, who's playing secret agent trying to do my job.*

Her eyes narrowed. Hanson was right about one thing: all roads led to someone inside TZC.

While Arnold Zero was her odds-on favorite for bad guy
of the year, it didn't add up. Zero might have been a miniature
megalomaniac who, from her dealings with him in the past,
envisioned himself as sole ruler of the world.

So far she hadn't found any connection between Zero and the
B.U.T.T.S., but he could still be a solider working for them. The
B.U.T.T.S. often contracted out evil, and Zero was evil to the core,
but he hated working for others, even really bad others. After the
courts cleaned out his bank accounts as reparations for his many
criminal acts he was flat, busted broke. Could he be doing this for the
money? But where was the profit in releasing the zombies?

"I was hoping to find my father by now."

Hanson's words surprised her. Aloha nodded. "Do you know
where he is?"

Hanson's brown eyes drifted to hers. His lips formed a thin line,
and his brow wrinkled. "You're going to think I'm nuts."

Aloha grinned. "Listen, I've seen a lot of strange stuff in my
time as a L.I.P.S. agent. Most of it would be classified as weird to
normal folks, so frankly there is very little chance anything you tell
me is going to make me think you're nuts. And besides you're *wayyy*
too handsome to be nuts."

Hanson's cheeks flushed crimson, but he didn't seem unhappy
with the description.

Hanson cleared his throat. "I believe the people who have been
sucked into the fourth wall through cracks in the dome are trapped in
another realm, and somehow the scientists at TZC can see into this
other realm."

Aloha's mouth formed a lopsided grin. "Yup, you're right; that
does sound nuts.

But I once travelled back in time in an abandoned amusement park ride time machine, so your explanation makes perfect sense, which means of course you and I are both nuts. What else?"

Hanson continued, "TZC has created technology that allows them to control where and when the cracks form in the dome."

Aloha's cheeks grew cold. This was bad, very bad. Someone had planned to grab Elvis's brother and poor Annie Oakley, and the disappearances were probably tests of this new technology. She suspected the disappearances were only the tip of the proverbial iceberg. She'd seen such things before and experience told her she was running out of time. It was time for the L.I.P.S. to take center stage and she was the agent to do it.

Chapter Twenty-One

NIGHT HAD FALLEN WHEN THEY ARRIVED in her car at a relatively unseen spot in the forest bordering one side of Totally Zip's property. From here Aloha could see there were no guards patrolling the area beyond the barbed wire fence that encompassed the compound.

No doubt the fence was electrified and the building access points alarmed. But Aloha Armstrong was the Woman from L.I.P.S., so there were no locks or fences that would keep her out when she wanted in.

She glanced at Hanson seated in the passenger seat next to her. "You ready for this?" The diner owner managed a slight nod, given he was cramped up like a human pretzel, but she saw the uncertainty in his eyes.

Aloha smiled to herself, then opened the car door and stepped out into the cool night air. Hanson did the same, closing the door gently behind him as she'd instructed on the drive over. Make no more noise than absolutely necessary, she told him. Covert operations required maximum stealth. Sometimes the electric car came in handy. *I may keep the thing after all.*

Hanson had donned a form-fitting black t-shirt and tight black jeans that hugged his perfectly shaped butt.

(They had stopped briefly at his house so he could change into clean clothes.) He looked positively yummy in all black, but she had a job to do.

It took all her concentration to shelf her growing feelings for this hunky, gentle, kind man. Her feelings would have to wait until her mission was complete. Even then she would likely be reassigned to another job by L.I.P.S. central relatively shortly after this one, so her budding romance with Hanson would end before it began.

Too bad, she thought.

Hanson's head snapped up, and he stared at her, his brow wrinkled. "Is something wrong?" he said in a harsh whisper.

Her lips curled slightly at the corners, and the corners of her eyes crinkled. "No," she whispered. "Let's go."

She had taken time to access the hidden compartment in her car where she kept her LI.P.S. battle gear. Thankfully she'd had the time to make the modifications to the car and store her gear or she'd be screwed right now without it.

Secured by Velcro around her waist, over her form-fitting one-piece black jumpsuit, she had a nylon belt with six pouches of various sizes containing her tools made by Dr. Oh.

When they got to the fence Aloha squatted next to it. Through her bodysuit her skin tingled due to the high-voltage electrical energy coursing through the steel wire of the fence. If bare skin touched the fence the resulting charge wouldn't allow time for regrets or second chances.

She pulled her rubber-lined gloves from where they were folded over her belt and slipped them on. She then ripped open the Velcro flap on one of the pouches and pulled out a cigar tube-shaped object reminiscent of a battery, only slightly larger.

While holding the object in the fingers of her right hand she held the object within two inches of the top of the fence then, with the thumb and index fingers of her other hand, twisted the bottom of the cylinder counter clock wise.

The tingling sensation stopped.

"What did you do?" asked Hanson.

Aloha glanced at him as she secured the device once again in its pouch. "Field damper. It interrupts the flow of the electricity to this section of fence for one minute." She looked at her watch. "We don't have much time. Put on those gloves I gave you."

She had a backup pair of insulated gloves in her kit, which she'd lent him. They'd be a little bit of a tight fit but should do the job. He nodded and managed to squeeze his strong hands into them.

Then, with her leading the way, they climbed the fence together and simultaneously dropped over, landing softly and soundlessly in the damp grass on the other side of the fence. Within a few seconds the hum returned and Aloha could feel the tingling sensation again.

Now they were in hostile territory. From this point on she'd use the hand signals she'd taught Hanson in a ten-minute crash course. She hoped he could remember them because they had to maintain absolute silence if they were going to succeed in infiltrating TZC's facility.

She didn't share with him her concern about there being no guards or dogs or other form of living security. It meant the security measures were entirely electronic. If she found them before they detected their presence then they had a chance of stopping them, but if they didn't...well, she didn't want to think about the ramifications.

She'd never failed on a mission (at least not completely, anyway), but there had to be a first time.

It was a universal law the odds dictated: as her number of missions increased the risks also increased.

Crouching low, she motioned with her right hand for him to follow her. It pleased her when he nodded. He looked handsome with his face dirty with dark makeup to cut the glare in case there were spotlights. She fully expected there to be pressure plates hidden in the ground that once stepped on would trigger external lights.

She reached into one of the other pouches on her belt and pulled out a device the size and shape of a cell phone. She pressed the side with her gloved thumb and a small LCD screen lit up with a soft green glow.

The device was designed to detect metal objects emitting any background radiation or electrical impulses. She first swept the area ahead of them, and sure enough the tiny screen had found two pressure plates, one to their right, the other to their left, indicated by red markers on the screen. And there was a clear path between the plates.

She smiled to herself. *Thank you, Dr. Oh.*

She started moving slow but steady toward the building. She found the plates were in layered non-concentric circles all the way to the massive building. They reached a high blank wall with no windows and one thick steel door.

Next to the door was a proximity card reader pad. Without Dr. Oh's gadgets this would normally have been the end of the mission. Prox card readers were virtually unbeatable.

Even if you did manage to break through the thick steel door, prox card readers were usually connected to computers that would, at the least, record the intrusion or, at the best (for the *break-inee* not the *break-iner*), set off a surveillance camera. Then you'd be all over YouTube in ten seconds or less.

But never fear, Dr. Oh is here.

Aloha placed the energy detector in its pouch and pulled out the universal key generator. It was the thickness of a credit card and about the same size and shape. Within its millimeter thick surface was the smallest, most sophisticated computer ever built. It was thumbprint activated to the user. It couldn't be hacked or operated by any unauthorized personnel – but that didn't include the Woman from L.I.P.S.

Aloha removed a glove, then pressed her thumb lightly against the back. She then swiped it across the prox card reader. There was a barely audible click as the door lock disengaged. She glanced at Hanson, who nodded, obviously impressed with her skills.

And who wouldn't be?

After putting away the computer card she put back on her glove then very carefully pressed the door open with the flat of her hand. It swung inward soundlessly. *I'm so glad they oil their hinges.* She placed the card back in its pouch and then pulled out the scanner again.

Hanson took a step toward the open door, but Aloha stopped him with one hand on his muscular abdomen. *Hello, six pack. Nice.*

She looked into his hazel eyes and shook her head. He nodded he understood. She turned back to the open door and swept the area beyond the door.

Good. No trip wires, no pressure plates, no indication of electrical surveillance or radiation other than that of the standard background variety. Could it really be this easy? Now she was really worried.

With a nod of her head to Hanson she stepped through the door and now stood in a long carpeted hallway that ran to a glass door. The glass in the door was smoked, so she couldn't see what lay beyond. Hanson stepped in after her.

She indicated he should close the steel door behind them, which he did.

A strange odor permeated the air causing her nose to wrinkle. The smell reminded her of over-ripe bananas.

On either side of the hallway at regular intervals were plain wood doors with numbers on them starting from 100 on the door closest to them.

They started moving down the hallway side by side, Aloha holding the scanner out just in case. The sound of something rattling stopped them in their tracks. Aloha quickly located where the sound came from. Someone was going to enter the hallway from the door numbered 111.

Oh, crap. She looked around. They only had a second or two at most. She stepped to the closest door, and then used the computer lock to open it. The door swung open revealing pitch-blackness beyond. There was no time but to choose what was behind door number 106.

After ushering Hanson inside she stepped in and quickly closed the door behind them. She put away the card, then reached into another pouch on her belt and pulled out a flashlight.

This was a very special flashlight capable of turning night into day. This meant they wouldn't have to turn on a light switch, but they would still be able to see the entire room.

She engaged the light by pressing a button recessed into the bottom of the flashlight, and the room lit up.

She blinked as her eyes adjusted to the sudden intrusion of light, then her jaw dropped in astonishment at what she was seeing. There was an empty desk nearby so she set the light upright on it, the light splashing across the white painted ceiling, illuminating the room.

Along one wall were large steel tubes with glass fronts. The tubes contained human bodies. And if she knew her gray dead pallor (which she did, since she'd dated someone with it in a past life) these were zombie bodies. Dead zombie bodies.

Aloha stepped closer to the nearest (she couldn't stop thinking of them as coffins) tube and studied the male figure inside. He seemed familiar. Her eyes narrowed.

She pulled out the computer card, activated it, and scanned the face of the body in the tube with a swipe. The computer was capable of scanning through the glass and would capture the DNA information and then transmit it to Wally back at L.I.P.S. HQ. After running it through the L.I.P.S. worldwide network he'd identify the person. Wally would send the results of his investigation to her on a coded narrow beam message to the communication node also on her belt.

Moving to the next tube Aloha did a scan with the computer card over its occupant. He looked familiar as if she were having a déjà vu experience. She froze when she heard Hanson draw in a sharp breath from behind her.

She turned and faced him and saw his face had paled. His eyes were wide. She decided to break the silence. "What?" she whispered.

"That's my father," he breathed, his eyes watery, his lower lip trembling.

Chapter Twenty-Two

ALOHA PEERED THROUGH THE GLASS at the face of the older man. His gray hair was thin on his smooth head, and his face was lined with age wrinkles, and there were laugh lines around the thin-lipped mouth and the closed eyes.

Aloha's heart froze.

This man was once a real person. Someone had robbed him of the precious gift of life. Her jaw tightened.

Her mind was made up. That someone would pay for these crimes.

It dawned on her now where she'd seen him before. This was indeed her predecessor, Sheriff Bradley. If it wasn't him, then he certainly was the spitting image of the man Wally had shown her in the file photo.

Her eyes narrowed. If this were a trick, then the DNA scan would reveal the truth. She turned around to face Hanson. He wasn't faring well. This gray-haired man appeared to be Hanson's father, but until it was confirmed one way or the other she had to take care of him. Aloha needed to help the diner owner keep it together. She couldn't have him go postal at this critical juncture.

But his eyes were red, and his cheeks had trails left behind by tears.

Not good. Not good at all. "Listen, Hanson, I know that man looks like your dad, but I'm having Wally check the DNA. Before we jump to any conclusions let's wait for the test results, OK?"

Hanson's features brightened a little, which suggested at least some of what she said had slipped through his grief shields. He didn't say anything but slowly nodded his head.

She stiffened when the encrypted communicator in the pouch on her right side vibrated against her hip. Wally had worked fast this time. Good and bad, the opposing twins in any situation.

There was no point in delaying things. Bad news was impossible to avoid. Delay, sure but never completely avoid. She hoped it was good news, but that would only be good for Hanson, not necessarily for the world.

If the news were good for him it would mean someone was creating zombies that resembled other people. And if this were true, then the consequences meant someone had a plan, and not a good plan. She would have to stop this before it got started.

If the body were a fake, the duplicate sheriff would have to be... Aloha didn't want to dwell on what she might have to do, but she was convinced this wasn't the real article.

Truthfully all she wanted to think about right now was the current situation in front of her. She had enough to deal with without having to dry some guy's eyes.

She paused and chastised herself for being so insensitive. The man could be Hanson's father. Just because she and her dad hadn't spoken in twenty years didn't mean Hanson had the same broken relationship with his father.

After placing a hand on his shoulder she looked him in the eyes, and her mouth formed a gentle smile. "It'll be OK," she whispered softly. "I'll take this call and find out the truth."

She locked eyes with him. "Please trust me. I will tell you the truth no matter what, OK?"

Something behind Hanson's eyes told her he trusted her, and the way the tension drained from his broad shoulders as they relaxed confirmed what she saw. She pulled out the communicator and lifted it to her mouth. She spoke softly into the tiny receiver. "Alpha seven, one, one, banana, two."

She then held the device away and looked at the tiny screen. The confirmation code flashed, then the screen changed and two names appeared.

Billy Morton and Axel Bradley. The first zombie was a member of the skateboard zombie boys; the other was indeed Sheriff Bradley. She glanced up from the screen at Hanson. She knew she had to tell him, but she didn't want to. Like her, Hanson had come to Zomopolis to find Bradley, and now he and Aloha had, but they were too late. Sheriff Bradley was dead.

The communicator beeped, and she glanced at the screen again. The words had changed. Only one name showed now, it was Bradley with the word alive right after it.

Her heart seemed to freeze in her chest. He wasn't dead.

Aloha stuffed the communicator in its pouch, then rushed up to the tube. She began to run her hands over the smooth surface looking for a latch or button to open it.

"What?" asked Hanson.

"He's alive," she breathed then, realizing what she'd just said and what it meant, she jerked her body around to look at the diner owner, whose face registered shock and understanding simultaneously. He rushed over to the glass tube. Together they began to search for the lock or latch or some other way of getting into the tube.

Aloha stopped and felt like slapping her forehead with the palm of her hand. The computer key card could defeat any locking mechanism, but she wasn't sure she should open the thing. If the sheriff was near death, then Hanson would want to save him, delaying their mission and possibly resulting in them being caught and maybe even getting them all killed.

If they were dead, then who would complete the mission? Besides she sensed time was limited. Any delay, even a few precious seconds, might mean failure not only for them but also for the world. Another agent couldn't possibly take over for her. There wasn't time, and she knew it. She didn't know how she knew, she just did.

If the zombies got loose then this time the outside world might not be able to stop them. Zombies had been contained for decades. Sure a few were seen outside the dome on occasion, but small numbers were manageable and contained quickly. Every year a few were captured and sent to Zomopolis where there now lived as many as a thousand of the undead.

If the brain eaters and the veggie zom's got loose on an unsuspecting population and their groceries eaten quickly. Too quickly. No, she had to stop Blind Bill, or maybe Arnold Zero, before they destroyed the world.

"Uhhh, Hanson, he might be infected. If we open the door without checking him carefully, and taking precautions, we'll be risking not only my mission but also life on the planet, as we know it, including ours. Face it, if we die, then what good are we to him," with a tilt of her head she indicated the body in the tube, "and to those outside Zomopolis depending on us to protect them from these undead monsters."

Aloha swallowed hard and cringed inside at those last two words.

She had friends who used to be half-zombies, and they certainly weren't monsters. But zombies suggested Zero's involvement. He'd tried to take over the world using the undead before. She'd stopped him then and she was determined to stop him again.

This operation the megalomaniacs tiny fingerprints all over it, but so far he'd come up clean, and that bothered her. She wanted Zero behind bars where all power mad wannabe despots belonged.

"What about that scanner on your belt. Can it detect germs or something that would show us if it were safe to open the tube or not?" he asked.

Aloha stared at him for several seconds as she considered his suggestion. She sighed. He was right. Wally would be able to tell from the scan data if the body was infected.

She pulled out her communicator then entered a text message. She wanted to keep verbal communications as limited as possible.

It didn't take long for Wally to respond. The body was clear of any infection or unusual chemicals. Aloha had almost hoped Sheriff Bradley had been carrying some disease. If he turned out to be a zombie or near zombie, then it might get ugly fast. The last thing she wanted to do was shoot a man's father in the head right in front of his son. But she would if it came to that.

Now they had to find a latch or catch to get this thing open. She glanced uneasily down the row of tubes each containing an immobile zombie. If they found something to open this door, then it might open all of them. If that were the case then they could be in real trouble, fast.

"Do you see any lock or something we can use to open this?" said Hanson running his hand along the edge of the tube where the glass abutted the metal case. There didn't seem to be any signs of even hinges.

Odd. "No, but there has to be some; they got into the tubes..." Aloha's voice trailed off as her eyes traveled above the tube to the ceiling.

A stainless steel track ran across the ceiling above the tubes stopping just before the top of the doorframe. She followed the track back the other way to the opposite wall. Surprisingly it disappeared in a square hole in the wall larger than the track. In fact it was far larger, wide enough for a man to go through lying in a horizontal position. She had a bad feeling about this setup.

"I think I know how this works," she said. Hanson stopped and looked at her. She pointed to the track above the row of tubes using her index finger to follow the track until it disappeared into the wall.

Hanson frowned. "So there's another room on the other side of the wall?"

Aloha nodded. "I would say so, but I suspect this room is where they store the zombies after whatever goes on in that room. I've seen zombie making before and this lab looks exactly like the one I've seen."

Hanson's cheeks paled. "So they create them there, then store them here." Aloha nodded. "That means if my dad isn't a zombie yet, he soon will be."

Aloha's heart ached for him. She had to restrain herself from wrapping her arms around him and hugging him. "So it would seem," she said softly.

Since his father was not registering as a full zombie, Hanson had to be right. The zombie-making process had to be in multiple stages. And this room had to be where the final stage took place. It was at this moment Aloha decided this place had to be destroyed. The entire world was at risk if someone could make zombies.

Chemical accidents and voodoo spells were bad enough; they had twelve step programs for those zoms, but some evil genius making them to dominate the planet. *Not on my watch they don't.*

Hanson's features darkened, and his brow wrinkled, and his eyes narrowed. "Then we have to open the top of dad's tube and get him out of there before he's fully zombie."

Aloha nodded. There must be some sort of suspended animation gas in the tube, but she only had one gas mask on her belt.

She cursed herself for not planning ahead for this eventuality. Her mistake meant one of them would have to wait in the hallway. And that was risky, very risky.

If the guard came by while she or Hanson waited outside until the all-clear signal was given ...she hesitated, not wanting to think of the possible ramifications.

She made her decision. She pulled the gas mask from its pouch and handed it to Hanson. He locked eyes with her. "Put this on before you open the tube. I expect gas will be released once you open the top. It shouldn't take long to dissipate."

She next handed him Dr. Oh's scanner. "The scanner will register the gas and will signal you with a beep when it's safe to remove the mask." She turned away and headed for the door to the hallway beyond. "I'm going to wait in the corridor until you give the all-clear signal."

"Why not you? You're the secret agent."

She grinned. "He's your father, not mine."

Hanson accepted the mask from her. It was on the small side, really designed by Dr. Oh for her, but should've been large enough to cover his mouth and nose. The head strap would hold the form-fitted rubber seals around the nose and mouth snug enough to prevent leaks.

She hoped.

He tried to pull it on, but the straps were too tight. Aloha took it from him and adjusted the straps. After she gave it back to him he pulled it on easily over his head covering his mouth and nose. Aloha stepped behind him and adjusted the straps until she was satisfied no gas would get in.

She moved around to the front of him and saw Hanson's eyes were watering. "Too tight?" she asked.

He nodded. "Yes," he said, his voice muffled by the mask. His features were distorted.

Aloha chuckled to herself. *I think I overdid it.* But she couldn't help herself; she had grown very fond of him and would hate it if anything happened to him.

"Sorry." She moved behind him again to loosen the straps a little. "Better?" He nodded, his eyes smiling at her over the nosepiece. "Good."

Aloha went to the door. "I'll be in the hallway."

Without looking back, she opened the door a crack and listened carefully for any sounds of movement. Hearing no echo of footsteps, she stepped out, closing the door behind her.

Sagging back against the wall, Aloha let out a deep sigh. The stress in this spy business could really wear a person down some days.

She started when the echo of someone turning a door lock filled the silent hallway, and her heart rate increased until it pounded in her chest so hard she thought it might burst out of her skin any second.

Someone was coming. It had to be the guard.

Her eyes flitted to the doorknob beside her. She had to stay where she was so Hanson could finish getting his father out of the tube.

If the guard saw her enter the room he'd follow her and find Hanson. Then all would be lost.

Oh, crap this could be the end of the line. *My last mission.*

Chapter Twenty-Three

ALOHA SUCKED IN A BREATH when two doors down from where she stood the door opened and Arnold Zero entered the hallway.

His beady eyes went wide when he saw her standing there in a skin-tight black bodysuit. His eyes locked on the small pistol she held in her right hand, the barrel pointed at him.

"Huh...Agent Armstrong...how did you get here?"

"Hands up, Zero."

Zero complied.

Aloha noticed he'd left the door open. *Interesting.* "And no funny business, or you're gonna leak when you drink a glass of water." She walked to stand over him, and then shoved him face-first against the wall.

He grunted.

"Assume the position," she said sharply, emphasizing her words with a tap of the gun barrel against his back.

Zero had spent time in prison, so he knew the drill. He stepped back, and then leaned into the wall spread-eagling his arms and legs.

After patting him down for weapons and finding none, she questioned him. "What are you doing here this time of night?"

Zero stood up straight and dropped his arms to his sides. "I could ask you the same thing," he said, the trace of arrogance returning to his voice.

Aloha stuck the gun into the middle of his back making him draw in a breath. One side of Aloha's mouth curled upward slightly. After all he'd done to her and many of her friends, subjecting him to a little discomfort didn't seem completely out of line.

Then it occurred to her she was the sheriff of Zomopolis. She had an obligation, an oath, to be better than him and people like him. Her fight was in the service of good not evil. Reluctantly she withdrew the gun barrel from the little man's back.

"Thank you, Agent," said Zero with a sigh.

"You're welcome. Now, please tell me why you're here."

Zero turned to face her. "I work here, for one thing, but more importantly I want to stop a mad man before he destroys the world."

~~~

Aloha gave her head a shake and lowered her gun to her side. She could not believe what she was hearing.

Arnold Zero, the little megalomaniac she first met on a reality show (she'd heard of him before the show, but never met him, and was sorry when she did), had tried to kill her and her friends the first time she'd met him.

Now he wanted to save the world. *Big HUH?*

"Really," said Zero. His cheeks were rosy, and his brown eyes were clear. He was serious and appeared truthful.

"Ok, but that doesn't explain why you're here this late at night." Aloha raised her gun again and trained it on him.

Zero sighed. "I'm looking for the key to that door behind you."

Aloha considered his words. On the one hand if she told him she already had the door open he would walk in on Hanson rescuing his father. On the other hand, if he were telling the truth, then he might be able to help them stop whoever or whatever was behind the plot to let loose the zombies.

On the other hand... Aloha paused to look at her hands. She only had the two she came with. Her options were limited.

"Are there any guards I should be worried about?"

Zero shook his head and opened his mouth to speak when Aloha interrupted him. "Good. Follow me."

She turned around, opened the door, and saw that Hanson had his father out of the tube and seated on the floor. The gas must have dissipated enough because he had his gas mask off. He sat on the floor beside his father and was patting his right cheek trying to wake him. But Sheriff Bradley was unconscious. Aloha suspected he wouldn't wake easily.

Hanson looked up as the door opened. His eyes were watery and drooped at the corners. Her heart beat harder at seeing how Hanson was hurting. She shook off the feeling. She had a job to do; too much was at stake.

"What's wrong with him?" she said to Zero. The little man frowned.

Oh, crap he has no idea.

"We have to find the antidote."

Hanson looked up from trying to wake his father by alternately patting his right then his left cheek. The old man's pale flesh had begun to glow a soft crimson.

"Where is it?" he asked, his tone desperate.

Zero nodded at the door at the other end of the room and the line of zombie-filled tubes.

"Behind that door is the creation lab." He lowered his voice, and his tone became deadly serious. "But I warn you, you will not like what you see."

Hanson stood up, his fists clenched at his sides so tight his knuckles were white. "I'm ready; let's go."

Aloha moved to stand in front of him. Placing one hand flat on his chest she locked eyes with him. "Listen, Hanson, I have experience in these things so I know Zero isn't exaggerating. Whatever we find will be horrible."

Hanson peered around her at Zero. "That's Zero?"

She couldn't help herself, a whisper of a smile played across her lips.

"Yes," she said simply.

His eyes flitted to her. "I don't care about any of that. I want to save my father. That's all I care about right now."

Aloha wanted to draw him to her and hug him, but instead she patted the side of his arm and smiled. "Ok, but remember I warned you."

Zero chose this moment to interrupt them. He walked up and stood beside them with his arms crossed and his eyes brimming with anger. "How're are we going to get in?"

Aloha glanced at the small man, as a tight smile formed on her lips. "No worries about that."

~~~

As soon as they entered, bright lights flooded the room forcing them to squint. Aloha froze as she heard the faint whirr of a motor for a surveillance camera. Under her breath she cursed herself. She should have thought of this. But until now it all seemed too easy.

No guards, doors that opened too easily and the only living persona a three-foot-six-inch megalomaniac who claimed to be working for the good guys for a change. The leopard had changed its spots, and she didn't believe it. At least not yet.

Aloha raised one hand to shield her eyes and drew in a breath when she saw the bodies laid out on tables before them. The one nearest to her was the missing forewoman, Annie Oakley.

"Hanson," she said in an urgent whisper. "Do you see Elvis's brother?"

"Yes," he said grimly. "He's on the third table from the end, second row."

Aloha counted sixteen tables in all. Sixteen humans were being zombified. Someone at TZC was creating zombies not curing them.

"Why, Sheriff, and Mr. Braddock, how nice to see you. And you too, Mr. Zero."

Aloha blinked, and out of the shadows stepped Blind Bill bookended by two zombies built like WWE wrestlers.

Aloha glanced at Hanson. "You know these two?" She indicated the two wrestler types with a nod of her head.

"Yes. Peter and Orville Light. They were part of The Fourth Wall 2 Live Crew until they disappeared four months ago."

Aloha's jaw dropped. "How many people disappeared through the dome wall?"

Hanson shrugged. "Twenty-seven. At last count."

Why didn't someone tell me before now? It's called a clue, people! And a big one.

"Something wrong?" asked Hanson.

Blind Bill doffed his dark glasses to reveal his eyes; one green and one blue, and stepped forward. He crossed his arms and chuckled grimly.

"I believe Agent Armstrong is a little peeved at the residents of a town where secrets run deep and information is withheld. Isn't that correct, Agent?" Aloha snapped her head around to look at Bill's sneering narrow features and glaring eyes. He looked directly into Aloha's eyes.

"Where's Elvis?" she said.

Bill smirked; his eyes flitted to a row of glass tubes that ran the length of the room then back to her. "Alive. For now. He'll be joining my zombie army very soon alongside his former boss."

Bill knew who she was, which meant one thing. "You work for the B.U.T.T.S., don't you, Bill?"

The know-it-all grin on his face faded. His brow wrinkled, and his eyes narrowed. He glanced side to side at the zombies standing on either side of him.

"Kill them." He paused to look at Zero. "Him as well."

Bill turned and walked away. His footstep's echoes disappeared when a door opened and closed.

She heard the sound of a deadbolt being slid into place, which meant they were alone with the two muscular brain-eaters. At least she assumed they were brain-eaters, given they were created in this lab. Chemical zoms were all brain-eaters.

What good would the B.U.T.T.S. have for vegetarian zombies... *hold on*. If they unleashed vegetarian zombies on the world, no one would care until it was too late.

They'd eat up all plants, flowers, and vegetables, clearing the land like locusts until it was too late.

She suspected the B.U.T.T.S. had cornered the market on plant seed and once the zombies starved and died they'd take over and offer the seeds to the highest bidder. A vegetarian take over plan was genius. They'd control the world.

Truly a terrible plan too awful to contemplate.

"They're vegetarians," Aloha said.

"What?" asked Hanson, backing up to the door to the outer lab. He tried the doorknob, and it was locked. His voice raised an octave. "How do you know?"

Aloha looked at the diner owner grimly. "It makes perfect sense. They'll lull the world into a false sense of security with the veggie zom's until they corner the plant seed market and thus all the vegetables and fruit in the world. It's an incredibly simple yet devious plan."

The two zombies raised their arms, extending their hands like claws and began to slowly circle Aloha, Hanson, and Zero, getting ever closer.

Aloha instructed Hanson and Zero to form a triangle shape with her, their backs to each other. She had a secret weapon just for the occasion. Dr. Oh to the rescue once again.

She pulled the sprayer out of the pouch on her belt and aimed it at the zombie getting close to her. Its outstretched fingers were inches from her when she pulled the trigger.

The cloud of mist quickly enveloped the zombie's head. It stopped moving and blinked, then began to scream and stumbled backward covering its face with its hands. Finally it thumped hard into the wall and collapsed to the floor unconscious. Aloha quickly sprayed the other zombie who was also unconscious within seconds of application.

"Wow! What's in the sprayer?" asked Zero.

"It's a mixture of highly concentrated vegetable oil and a new and improved Zombie Away formula," Aloha replied.

"Where did you get that?"

She sheathed the spray canister in its pouch and looked at Zero. "That's classified information you don't need to know."

Zero shrugged.

Hanson waved his hand at the room full of half-made zombies. "What do we do now?"

Aloha placed her hands on her hips, her pale face split by a wide grin. "We set them free and destroy all this equipment, naturally."

"By ourselves?" protested Hanson.

"No. We call in the cavalry."

Aloha pulled out her communicator. "Wally?"

"Yes, Agent Armstrong."

"Give Elvis a call. Tell him to call Billy Buick. We'll need his entire team to clean this place."

"Yes, Agent."

"And make sure you tell him everything you heard over the open COM link."

"Of course, Agent Armstrong." She then cut the link and turned to face Hanson and Zero.

"Boys, it's payback time."

Chapter Twenty-Four

IT TOOK THREE DAYS, but with the help of the Fourth Wall 2
Live Crew they had all of the illegal laboratory equipment
dismantled and burned to ashes. No one would ever manufacture
zombies at TZC again.

Aloha and the mayor met with the CEO and his staff about the
activities of Blind Bill. They claimed they had no knowledge of him
or the B.U.T.T.S., but Aloha had her suspicions. TZC was involved
in top-secret research—a perfect cover for the B.U.T.T.S.

She'd have to keep an eye on their operations. And on Arnold
Zero.

The little man was about to be killed by Bill's man-made
zombies and had helped them. He claimed he was innocent, and she
had no way of proving if he was involved in Bill's scheme.

Blind Bill, the B.U.T.T.S. agent, had disappeared. He'd be back,
and next time Aloha was determined to catch him. The L.I.P.S. agent
always got its man, woman, or whatever.

After the destruction was complete all the man-made zombies,
both those fully formed and those part way through the process, were
freed and returned to normal. The mayor even had a town holiday
and picnic planned to welcome them back from the undead.

Sharona was a good egg, but a bad artist. Aloha had seen her paintings and they were truly awful. Even though beauty was in the eye of the beholder, she'd have to have a jaundiced eye to like that crap.

~~~

Aloha sighed heavily as she slid into the booth at Hanson's diner. The handsome café owner came by with a coffee pot. "Hey, Sheriff. Coffee?"

Aloha nodded and turned over the cup in the saucer on the table in front of her.

"Tough day?" he said as he filled the cup to the brim.

She smiled at the realization he knew she enjoyed her coffee black. *I've been here far too long.* "Yeah, you could say that, Hanson. I just received my new orders."

She had extracted a promise from him not to tell anyone she was actually the Woman from L.I.P.S. working undercover. Of course it helped she'd saved his father from his undead fate, and his friends, too, of course.

"Leaving us so soon?" he said, his voice tinged with a trace of regret.

She raised the cup to her lips and took a sip of the warm brown liquid. The rich coffee played across her taste buds, until it disappeared down her throat. She chuckled after swallowing and lowering the cup to the saucer.

"Actually, no. Sharona asked me to stay on as Sheriff of Zomopolis." She shrugged. "You know, since your father decided to retire to Florida there is an opening." Hanson smiled. "What about you?"

He shrugged. "I kinda like it here. I think I'll stick around. Besides, who would buy a diner in a town full of zombies?"

Of course, it didn't help she'd not completed the red stake order, the first time in the history of the service. Director Mynass had yelled at her for twenty minutes until he calmed down and told her she could rot in Zomopolis as far as he was concerned. Even though she'd saved the world once again it would take time for the director to calm down and talk to her again. Oh, well, she decided she'd have to make the best of a bad situation.

Aloha looked at him, her eyes narrowing. "You up for dinner and a movie Friday?"

He nodded. "My place?"

"Yeah, sounds good." With that, he turned and walked away.

She watched him go, her eyes fixated on his tight buns. Gripping the cup in both hands, she raised it to her mouth her green eyes peering over the brim.

Yup, this is going to be some interesting job.

Aloha Armstrong will return in, *Zomopolis II: Mummy's Day*

About the Author

International selling author, Russ Crossley writes romance under the name R.G. Hart, mystery/suspense under the name R.G. Crossley, and science fiction and fantasy under his own. This year there will be re-issues the romantic comedies, Bachelorette: Zombie Edition by Champagne Books, and Antique Virgin by 53rd Street Publishing, paranormal romantic comedy, Zomopolis, and a new western romance entitled, The Fire In Their Hearts co-authored with R.S. Meger will be published in 2013 by Champagne Books. Also, look for another Aloha adventure, Bloody Betty Queen of the Pirates coming in the spring of 2013 from Champagne Books.

In addition the near future suspense novel, The Last Serial Killer by R.G. Crossley was recently released by 53rd Street Publishing in ebook and trade paperback versions.

He has sold several short stories that have appeared in anthologies from Pocket Books, St. Matins Press, at Smashwords, Amazon, and other e-retail sites.

With his wife, romance author R.S. Meger, he owns and operates a small press publishing company, 53rd Street Publishing. The company began in April 2011 and now has over one hundred e-book titles and a number of print titles, with more planned in 2012 and 2013.

He is a member of SF Canada and the Greater Vancouver Chapter of Romance Writers of America. He is also an alumni of the Oregon Coast Professional Fiction Writers Master Class taught by award winning author/editors, Kristine Katherine Rusch and Dean Wesley Smith.

To find a complete listing of his work check out his website http://www.rghart.com, http://russstory.blogspot.com.Razor's blog can be found at http://razorandedge.blogspot.com

Feel free to contact him on Facebook or Twitter. He loves to hear from readers

Other books by the Author

Titles as R.G. Crossley

Short Stories

Razor and Edge Mysteries
The Kidnapping of Billy Buttons
String of Pearls
Death by Clown
Beggin' For Murder
Ragged Ice
The Grand Central Mystery
A Strange Case of Undead Murder

Non-Series Mysteries
A Day Without Sunshine
Mirror Image
Dangerous Waters
Cape Disappointment
Boomerang
The Watcher of Wayburn Street
The Apprentice
Drip!
A Beautiful Friendship and The Parrot of Doom
Robine's Diary
The Christmas Club
Loose Ends
Skullduggery
Splatter Pattern
It Takes Two

Anthologies
The Adventures of Razor and Edge:
Five Tales From The Quirky Detective Team

Novels
A Bad Case of Loyalty
The Last Serial Killer
Shear Murder

Titles as Russ Crossley

Novels
Attack of the Lushites

Short Stories
Countdown
Shoeless Moe
Round Up At The Burger Bar:
The Story of Trixie Pug, Parts 1, 2, 3, 4, 5, 6
Five Minutes
Blossom Queen, Barbarian
The Secret
The Family Line
End of the Flies
With Death You Get the Eggroll
The Penguin Sleeps With The Fishes
Only The Worthy
Hero For A Day
End of Empire
Strange Bedfellows
Big Business
A Perfect Crime
The Wise Guy and The Pirates
In Search of the Perfect Cup
T.I.N. Men
The Legend of G and the Dragonettes
The Incredible Mr. Fix-It
Lock Stock and Barrel
Divided Loyalties
Cave of Wonders
A Family Empire

Until We Meet Again
Dragon Rising

Presents Anthology Series
Five Tales of Urban Fantasy
Five Tales of Bizarre Detectives
Five Tales of Mystery and Suspense
Five Tales of Weird Fantasy
Spies, Detectives, & Heroes
Tales of Twisted Crime
Five Tales of The Unexpected
Tales From Space
10 by Russ Crossley
Round Up At The Burger Bar: The Story of Trixie Pug,
Parts 1- 5 The Beginning
Worlds of Science Fiction and Fantasy
More Tales of Mystery and Suspense
Ladies of the Jolly Roger
Justice Served

Titles as R.G. Hart

Short Stories
Tikka's Big Day
"My Partner the Zombie" —
Hungry For Your Love Anthology
(St. Martin's Press)
Big Hairy Deal
One Red Shoe
A Bad Day in Lunden Texas
Hook Island
Grind Manor

Novels
Bachelorette: Zombie Edition
(from Champagne Books)
Antique Virgin

The Fire In Their Hearts
with R.S. Meger (coming soon from Champagne Books)
Zomopolis